"Anything with some Jane Austen flavor will always be a draw when it comes to female readers. And so the continuing saga of Sydney and her turn as a "modern-day Emma" in *Blessed Are the Meddlers* naturally piques my interest. I think readers will also enjoy this season of her life as Sydney attempts to help a sister out (literally) as well as play matchmaker with a couple of her friends. An enjoyable, realistic, and heartwarming read, to be sure!"

—LAURA MACCORKLE, senior editor, Crosswalk.com

"Christa Banister has her finger on the pulse of the modern young Christian single. Delightfully candid, *Blessed Are the Meddlers* unveils a witty and poignant view of believers struggling to find meaningful relationships and make a lasting impact on today's society. A warm, irresistible read for anyone desiring to move beyond garden-variety Christian chick lit and find grace-filled substance."

—DAVID MCCREARY, writer; editor

"Sydney is back on the scene, and she is funnier than ever. *Blessed Are the Meddlers* is even more enjoyable than *Around the World in 80 Dates*, which is the first novel by Banister. There are no fluffy characters or easy fixes in this story, and the relational conflicts are totally believable. Banister's voice is so unique. I've never read another author with similar flair and such a humorous take on things. The coolest part about *Meddlers* is you don't know whose relationship will work out and whose will fall flat. It's not easy to guess, either, and sometimes you'll discover the exact opposite of what you'd anticipated. But that is so like real life. Check out the latest saga from Christa Banister in *Blessed Are the Meddlers* and enjoy the ride."

—MICHELLE SUTTON, author of *It's Not About Me*

BLESSED ARE THE MEDDLERS

CONFESSIONS OF A SERIAL MATCHMAKER

CHRISTA ANN BANISTER

NAVPRESS®

NavPress is the publishing ministry of The Navigators, an international Christian organization and leader in personal spiritual development. NavPress is committed to helping people grow spiritually and enjoy lives of meaning and hope through personal and group resources that are biblically rooted, culturally relevant, and highly practical.

For a free catalog go to www.NavPress.com
or call 1.800.366.7788 in the United States or 1.800.839.4769 in Canada.

ISBN-13: 978-1-60006-178-3
ISBN-10: 1-60006-178-8

Cover design by The DesignWorks Group, Tim Green, www.thedesignworksgroup.com
Cover photo by Steve Gardner, PixelWorks Studio
Author photo by Jessica Folkins

This novel is a work of fiction. Names, characters, places, and incidents are either the product of the author's imagination or are used fictitiously. Any resemblance to actual events, locales, organizations, or persons, living or dead, is entirely coincidental and beyond the intent of either the author or publisher.

Unless otherwise identified, all Scripture quotations in this publication are taken from the HOLY BIBLE: NEW INTERNATIONAL VERSION® (NIV®). Copyright © 1973, 1978, 1984 by International Bible Society. Used by permission of Zondervan Publishing House. All rights reserved.

Library of Congress Cataloging-in-Publication Data

Banister, Christa Ann, 1976-
  Blessed are the meddlers : confessions of a serial matchmaker /
Christa Ann Banister.
    p. cm.
  ISBN 978-1-60006-178-3
  1. Chick lit. I. Title.
  PS3602.A637B56 2008
  813'.6--dc22
                              2008010260

Printed in the United States of America

1 2 3 4 5 6 7 8 9 10 / 12 11 10 09 08

To all the single girls still waiting for Prince Charming . . .
this story is for you.

ACKNOWLEDGMENTS

I would also like to thank:

- Will, the best husband a girl could ask for. All of my dreams came true when we said "I do." Thanks for all your love and continued encouragement in everything. I love you.

- My family—Mom, Casey, Lindsey and Shayne and their precious baby M. I love all of you dearly.

- My extended family—the Banisters (Bill, Jo Ann, and Bess) and the Wilks (Louella and Don). Thank you so much for being so excited and supportive of *Around the World in 80 Dates*! I hope you enjoy this one even more.

- My incredible friends—life is all the richer because you're a part of it. Thank you Krista, Tracey, Kat, Janet, Katie, Suzie, Jessica, Melissa, and Wendy Lee for always being there and staying in touch even when life gets incredibly busy. You're also the best publicists in the world; thank you for all your joyful enthusiasm!

- To each and every one of my freelance clients — thanks for keeping me gainfully employed in the comfort of my pajamas. You rocketh!

- To Jamie, my trusty editor. Thank you for helping me make my thoughts less cluttered and for such fantastic dev edit notes. I couldn't have done this without you.

- To all the kind folks at NavPress, thank you for your support and excitement about my novels.

- And to Kathleen, who recovered my manuscript at the Apple Store in Roseville that horrible day, a giant thank you for your patience and computer know-how.

- Finally, thank you to Jesus, who makes life actually have meaning. I'm so grateful to you for each and every blessing.

CHAPTER 1

It's like that book I read in the 9th grade that said "'tis a far better thing doing stuff for other people."

— CHER HOROWITZ (ALICIA SILVERSTONE) IN *CLUELESS*, 1995

PEOPLE TELL ME I'M a modern-day Emma.

Of course, I've never worn a corset (thank goodness) or particularly cared for taking tea with those cute little cucumber sandwiches. I'm actually more like the Emma that Alicia Silverstone played in *Clueless*: a relatively well-dressed, modern girl with a sunny disposition and a weakness for wanting to help make people happy — especially in love.

Now that I am happily hitched, I take it as my solemn duty to make sure all my girlfriends are paired up too. After all, when I was hopelessly single, there were times when I could've used a major relationship intervention. So that's where I come in. I'm like eHarmony without the pesky questionnaire and quarterly payments. Or that persistent aunt who's always trying to fix you up with, oh, her tennis instructor. And unlike either of the aforementioned, I offer the personal insight of a trusted friend. Who can argue with that?

My most recent adventures in matchmaking started a couple

of months after I married the love of my life, Gavin, and officially became Mrs. Sydney Williams (née Alexander). I was sipping strawberry shortcake smoothies with my friend Jane after our weekly Pilates class. New to the Twin Cities after accepting a job as an on-air reporter at KARE-11, Jane and I had bonded immediately. Not only do we both work in journalism (I'm a full-time freelance writer and aspiring novelist), but we also attend the same church and share a mutual dislike for Pilates, despite its obvious benefits.

On the surface, Jane is one of those enviable women who seems to have everything going for her. She has flawless skin that glows without a single drop of Clinique, and her silky blonde hair is cut in an effortlessly chic, Victoria Beckham (aka Posh Spice) bob. Her workout clothes are even impeccably selected, black-and-white Juicy Couture sweats with robin's egg blue accents that bring out the unusual color of her eyes. Despite her exquisite taste in, well, just about everything, Jane hasn't been as lucky in love. And with my past experience of having gone on every bad date imaginable before meeting Gavin — unfortunate stories to which Jane could relate all too well — I desperately wanted to help. So after her initial uneasiness about yet another blind date, I set her up with Weston, the lone single guy in my hubby's touring band.

From what I could tell, Weston seemed normal enough. Sure, he only owned three T-shirts that he wore in a predictable rotation (the Police reunion tour shirt always came first, then his vintage Led Zeppelin, followed by a fading, slightly torn Foo Fighters tank top circa 1997). Another red flag was the winsome flakiness that often goes hand in hand with his choice of occupation. But what Weston did have going for him was a great deal of charm, a killer smile, and enviable chops as a drummer. In fact, Gavin says he's one of the best that he's *ever* worked with—and trust me, Gavin is particular about his drummers, *very* particular. Unfortunately Weston wasn't nearly as adept at keeping time with his own life. He was always running at least twenty minutes late. But as far as truly heinous flaws go (i.e., the crucial deal breakers that Jane and I agreed upon, including long stretches of unemployment, bad manners, extreme commitment phobia, issues with cleanliness, severe Mommy attachment, or a surplus of chest hair), Weston was in the clear. Or so we thought.

"At first everything was going reasonably well," Jane said as we settled in at Jamba Juice the morning after her disastrous date. "He was twenty minutes late and wearing the Led Zeppelin T-shirt just like you predicted, but I planned for that. What I didn't plan for was when he asked if I'd like to see his feet. He kept insisting they were *really, really* cute."

"What? He wanted to show you his *feet*?" I asked, feeling slightly nauseated. Feet aren't exactly my favorite body feature—especially guys' feet, which tend to be far more unkempt. In my opinion, a good pedicure could benefit anyone, especially a nonmetrosexual male.

"We were eating guac and chips. I nearly lost my appetite," Jane said. "I said no *at least* three times, and he took off his socks and shoes anyway—*right there in the restaurant*! Apparently he's rather proud of his hairy hobbit feet."

"Ewww," I said. "That's disgusting."

"You're telling me," Jane said with the dramatic tone she typically uses in her news clips. "It only went downhill from there. He started talking about his pets."

"Really?" I asked curiously. "But I thought you loved animals."

"Well, I do," Jane began. "But apparently not the way Weston does. He has five dogs and three cats, and they all sleep in the same bed as him."

"Gross!" I said, wondering how in the world Gavin hadn't picked up on Weston's peculiar lifestyle. I mean, it's great that Weston is responsible enough to take care of eight pets and play the occasional out-of-town show. But he's definitely headed toward wacko zookeeper territory, not exactly an aphrodisiac.

"Yeah, and he told me precisely where each animal sleeps. Boo Boo, his calico cat, sleeps right by his head just like a human. His golden retriever, Pesto, lies next to Rosemary, his cocker spaniel, at the foot of his bed. And Nacho—"

"Nacho?" I asked quizzically.

"Yeah, Nacho, is another one of his dogs," she said matter-of-factly. "Bottom line: I can't deal with *that* many pets."

"So did the night get *any* better?" I asked sympathetically. I mean, how much worse could it get?

"A little. But only because I told him I needed to head home and feed my fish," Jane added with her trademark cackle. For the record: Jane's laugh is an interesting cross between Chandler's ex, Janice, from *Friends* and Cameron Diaz's California girl giggle that can be heard in any number of her movies. It's loud and distinct, but somehow Jane manages to make it endearing.

"Oooooh, that's cold!" I replied. "Guess you won't be seeing *him* again."

"Well, he still asked for my number," Jane said. "Can you believe that? He didn't sense that things weren't going well."

"That's unfortunate." I sighed. "Well, at least we can cross

Weston off your list of potential boyfriends."

"Yeah." She sighed back. "Who else can you set me up with, Syd?"

             ✻   ✻   ✻

And that's the funny thing about matchmaking. No matter how terrible a job I've done in the past, my friends (and even a few of my clients) just keep coming back for more. It's practically my second job, even though my success rate is highly suspect, probably in the neighborhood of, oh, one for forty. It's a good thing I'm not matchmaking on commission or I'd be poor — *really* poor.

Just when I thought I'd be taking an extended break from setting up my girlfriends with their most recent Mr. Wrong, one of them would quickly remind me of my greatest success as Cupid: the day I introduced my friend Rain to Stinky Nate, who is now her husband.

At first blush, it probably seems a little rude to call someone, let alone a friend, Stinky Nate. But Nate, a barista at my favorite downtown Minneapolis coffee shop, Moose & Sadie's, *is* stinky and couldn't care less. Much like Matthew McConaughey, he prefers the au naturel approach to personal hygiene. Basically, Nate's the guy who'd make any environmental activist's attempts to go green seem paltry in comparison. Nate showers only on special occasions (thank goodness he did on his wedding day, one of his few nonstinky moments) and doesn't wear cologne — or even deodorant for that matter. Inspired by the way cats, his calico in particular, clean up by licking themselves, he's been in constant pursuit of a more felinelike way to keep himself fresh. He hasn't succeeded, though, which makes him smell less than desirable. Especially in the sweat-soaked summer months, which were rapidly approaching.

But I knew Rain, a strict vegetarian who sews her own smock tops and only wears jewelry woven from hemp, would find someone like Stinky Nate simply irresistible. Of course, Rain maintained she wasn't looking for love. Whenever I'd suggest a setup, she'd remind me that she was a feminist who was more than happy to spend the majority of her free time in the company of her two favorite musicians, Billy Joel and Helen "I Am Woman" Reddy. She needed a man like a fish needs a bicycle, she said.

So I did it the old-fashioned way: I slyly introduced them when Rain and I met at Moose & Sadie's for breakfast before church one Sunday morning.

I'm pretty sure it was love at first sight, even though I'm not naturally inclined to believe in that sort of thing. Nonetheless, Rain and Nate totally hit it off and went out two days later (so much for swearing off men, huh?). And from the first wheat germ smoothie, their chemistry was palpable. Nate proposed a couple of years later (with an engagement ring made from hemp, natch), even though Rain had vowed she'd never marry.

Now that the stinky/hippie couple is married—and happily so—I'll admit that I can't help but feel pleased whenever I see them together. Same goes for my best friend, Kristin, and her current beau, Justin. Even though I went out with Justin first (and trust me, it's far less complicated in hindsight than it sounds), I encouraged Kristin to be patient with Justin when he was having trouble making up his mind early on, and it's paid off big-time. They're not only sublimely happy, but they're talking about getting engaged soon. Thinking about Kristin getting engaged makes me think of how much I miss her. Ever since she accepted a teaching job in Duluth, which is a little more than two hours away, I hardly ever see her, save for the occasional weekend visit.

Despite my successes and the ever-growing number of singles in my social circle, it doesn't necessarily mean I'm destined for the soul mate–finding business, no matter how many of my girlfriends try to convince me that it's my gift. But in the name of love, I'll always give it my best shot.

CHAPTER 2

THREE'S A CROWD — EVEN IN FAIRY TALES

> I have this theory of convergence, that good things always
> happen with bad things. I know you have to deal with them
> at the same time, but I just don't know why they have to
> happen at the same time. I just wish I could work out some
> schedule.
>
> —DIANE COURT (IONE SKYE) IN *SAY ANYTHING . . .*, 1989

A COUPLE OF DAYS LATER, on a dreary Monday afternoon,
Sydney's sister, Samantha, was frantically searching her sad
excuse for a closet (it's about the size of a small kitchen cupboard)
for her cubic zirconia tiara. Typically, Sam would never own such
a princessy accessory, except that she'd won it at a beauty pageant
back in high school and kept it as a reminder of her past Miss
America ambitions. Of course, now that she'd outgrown the phase
when Vaseline was required for a perfect smile and Preparation H
was applied to keep any under-eye bags at bay after late nights out
and about, the tiara always provided a good laugh. And tonight
it would actually come in handy as the perfect centerpiece for the
Cinderella costume she was wearing to Bethel University's annual
Spring Fling gala.

Samantha hates costume parties with a passion unless it's

Halloween. It's not dressing up that's the problem—that's the fun part. The part that seriously racks her brain is coming up with a clever, cost-effective costume. Now that she's dating her Prince Charming, however, the obvious option presented itself immediately: She'd be Cinderella, and Eli would be the dashing Mr. Charming.

After what seemed like a decade of unrequited flirting (it was actually three years, but it felt much, *much* longer to her oh-so-patient friends and family), Samantha and Eli had finally started dating just before she left for an internship in Europe the previous summer. Eli had initially worried that she'd run off with some devastatingly handsome French Casanova who'd woo her with his knowledge of fine wines and froufrou cuisine, but the exact opposite happened. Her time away solidified how much she cared about Eli all along and how thankful she was to finally be in a relationship with him. It was comfortable, like a cup of chicken noodle soup. And now that they were about to graduate, they wouldn't have to worry about the demands of having classes and way too much homework to do. When they were no longer busy sending out résumés, they could enjoy long, leisurely summer afternoons of soaking in the sun, playing golf (one of their favorite competitive sports), and drinking Frappuccinos over a frank discussion of their hopes and dreams for the future.

As Samantha continued the search for her tiara, she stumbled upon the packet of wedding pics that Sydney had sent her a few weeks after her wedding. Although Sam wished she could've been present when her sister said, "I do," she admired the spontaneity that enabled Sydney and Gavin to elope—something they'd decided to do while slow dancing at Rain and Stinky Nate's wedding. Truth be told, she'd never seen Sydney so happy as she was with

Gavin. And it showed through beautifully in Sydney's bright smile as she held Gavin's hand in one particularly picturesque shot in front of the Eiffel Tower at Paris Las Vegas. While the Vegas version of the Eiffel Tower was impressively to scale, Samantha was equally impressed that Gavin insisted that Sydney experience the real thing as soon as possible too. So three days after they got married, Gavin and Syd got their picture snapped in front of the real Eiffel Tower during their two-week European honeymoon that began in Paris and ended in Venice, a dream come true for her adventure-seeking sister and the handsome love of her life.

As Sam flipped through the rest of the pics, admiring the vintage gown Sydney borrowed for the ceremony and the obvious devotion she held for Gavin, Samantha began daydreaming about what she'd look like in that gorgeous dress. It was classic and chic in an Audrey Hepburn sort of way, which fit Sydney to a tee. And since the sisters shared similar tastes in, well, just about everything, Samantha assumed the dress wouldn't look too shabby on her either.

Snapping herself out of her 'til-death-do-us-part trance, Samantha carefully placed the wedding pics back in the envelope. Then, after digging through several more stacks of clothes, she finally spotted the tiara behind a pair of pink flip-flops. Examining it for rust or missing stones (it actually had neither—a huge relief), Samantha began mentally debating whether it would look better with her hair up or down, and after experimenting with a few different styles, she eventually twisted her hair into a loose French twist.

As she fastened the final bobby pin into place, her cell phone rang with the familiar ringtone she'd selected for Eli (appropriately, it was "their song," Keith Urban's "Once in a Lifetime"; Sydney teased her about it relentlessly, calling it cheesy and laughing hysterically whenever she heard it). She grinned and secretly hoped that she and Eli would join the happily married ranks of Sydney and Gavin in the not-so-distant future.

❊ ❊ ❊

Meanwhile, back at Sydney and Gavin's condo . . .

When I was single, it was always challenging to imagine what married life would actually be like. Of course, when you're so over the whole dating thing that you're seriously weighing the pros and cons of joining the local convent (Hey, it wouldn't be so bad to wear black and white every day, right? At least it's slimming!), you're prone to idealizing it—especially if you're the romantic type who has watched Hugh Grant get the girl in way too many movies. As time has worn on, though, I've quickly realized that my single-girl daydreams didn't even scratch the surface of how deliriously happy I am. And it doesn't get much better than enjoying one of life's simple pleasures—a quiet dinner together at home.

"Mmm, something smells delicious, my little Rachael Ray," Gavin said in his best faux Italian accent as he closed the front door and walked toward the kitchen. Wearing the black-and-white-striped apron I'd picked up on the Paris leg of our honeymoon, I was putting the finishing touches on the fettuccine Alfredo I'd whipped up—his favorite. I'll admit, getting married has definitely brought out my inner domestic goddess. While Gavin and I ate out constantly when we were dating, there's been something so rewarding about making something from scratch (or with a little help from the supermarket—I mean, who actually takes the time to press fresh pasta?) and enjoying it in the comfort of our cozy little condo.

"Can you believe that I got so wrapped up in the new song I was working on today that I forgot to eat lunch?" Gavin asked as he wrapped his arms around my waist and leaned in for a kiss. "I'm starving!"

Greeting his lips with my own, I dutifully resumed my stirring. Alfredo sauce is a finicky breed, after all, prone to burning if left unattended. "You poor thing, you must be hungry!" I said. "That must have been one incredible song if *you* forgot to eat."

"No kidding. But I'm really liking how this song is progressing," Gavin said excitedly. "It has these moody chords and such a catchy chorus, but we'll see what happens. You know how I am—"

"Yep, you've got to feel it," I said with a knowing smile. The funny thing about Gavin is that he isn't a perfectionist about most things. One look at his socks would tell you that. Although he only wears white, they rarely match. Not only are they different brands, but one is always much longer than the other. But he rationalizes that because he wears them under jeans, it doesn't really matter anyway. For him, the trouble of taking the time to match the socks offers far too little in return.

Of course, mismatched socks would drive a type A personality like me positively batty, but Gavin doesn't seem to mind—not in the least. His songs, however? That's an entirely different matter. Hands down, he is his own worst music critic. Sometimes he plays me songs that I'm sure will become a number one hit, and he nitpicks, saying a particular line is "too obvious" or that musically it sounds a little too much like (insert name of trendy British band here).

"So I guess you won't be playing the song for me until it's absolutely perfect," I said as I handed Gavin his plate of buttery pasta and fresh-from-the-oven garlic toast.

"Nope," Gavin said with a grin. "But I'm planning on finishing it this week, so maybe I'll have something to play for you soon. Fingers crossed."

"I hope so. You haven't played me anything new for a while," I said, playfully swatting his arm.

Turning his attention to his plate, Gavin said, "Patience, my love—*patience*. My brilliant song will just have to wait. Now about this dinner . . . what exactly are we celebrating tonight?"

With my best dramatic flair, I stood up and held my wine glass up high, like I was proposing a toast. I tapped the glass with my butter knife for emphasis and said, "Well, not only have we been married for sixty-three glorious days, but we're celebrating that I've finally figured out who I'm going to set Jane up with next."

"You mean she doesn't want to give poor Weston another chance?" Gavin replied with a laugh. "He keeps talking about her at band practice. Said she's the coolest girl he's met in a long time."

"Sorry. That's *sooo* not happening," I said, settling into my chair. "Somewhere between seeing his feet and hearing about his pet menagerie, she got the impression it wasn't going to work."

"Well, if it's not Weston, then who?" Gavin asked quizzically, flashing that shy, sexy smile I could never get enough of.

"I was thinking Campbell Smith, the new singles' pastor at church. Isn't he perfect?"

"Interesting choice," Gavin said. "But doesn't that sort of defeat the whole purpose of him being a singles' pastor? Isn't it

BLESSED ARE THE MEDDLERS

better if he's actually single? That way he's in the same boat as everyone else in the group."

"Or he could be the success story that gives everybody hope," I countered. "Don't you think he and Jane would be cute together? He's athletic just like she is, they're both extremely involved at church, and from what I've heard, he only has one dog."

"You've obviously given this some serious thought," Gavin teased as he twirled the long fettuccine strand around his fork. "Who knows, maybe they're a match made in heaven."

"No, that's only reserved for people who spot the love of their life on a transatlantic flight. Like I did," I replied flirtatiously. I thought about that blissful afternoon on a flight from London to Minneapolis when I saw "Mr. Hottie" for the first time. I didn't know his name was Gavin until a few months later when we officially—and unexpectedly—met at Moose & Sadie's. I'd been toiling over the daily Scrabble puzzle from the Minneapolis *Star Tribune*, and Gavin helped me figure out a four-letter word. *Dwam*, in case you're curious, which means "a daydream."

"Yeah, that *was* heavenly," Gavin said as he leaned over and squeezed my hand. "I'm not so sure Jane and Campbell could come close to topping that."

✳   ✳   ✳

Dancing the night away . . .

Unlike Samantha's disastrous prom experience back in high school—her date ignored her for the better part of the evening, and he had asked *her* (seriously, the nerve of some guys!)—she was actually enjoying herself at a school dance. Instead of the cheesy Party City décor cluttered with crepe paper streamers and far too many helium balloons to ever be considered chic, the setting for the Spring Fling gala was elegant in the manner of Old Hollywood. Samantha couldn't believe how the Bethel gymnasium had been magically transformed. Each "room," inspired by a different romantic movie, was nestled inside a large white tent, thin enough to see the twinkling stars that had been skillfully arranged into constellations on the ceiling.

The centerpiece of the *Casablanca* room was a vintage baby grand piano, where the player, regally dressed in a double-breasted tuxedo, quietly performed "As Time Goes By," the song that both haunted and enraptured the movie's lovers, Rick and Ilsa. Keeping the theme of complex relationships alive, the nearby *Roman Holiday* room was decorated in the rich rustic reds, greens, and yellows of Italy's countryside, with delicious bruschetta and prosciutto-wrapped veggie appetizers to match. A couple of tall Romanesque statues stood on each side of the long serving table where the food was displayed, while large Tuscan sunflowers arranged in slender gold vases added an earthy vibe.

While each room was beautiful in its own right, with exquisite attention paid to every detail, it was *The Notebook* room that really took Eli's and Samantha's breath away. In one corner of the room, sand covered the floor, and a canoe was propped on top of it, oars and all, giving it a beachy feel. In the opposite corner was an antique table and chairs set up for two, with a red rose draped on top of a leather-bound book with the words "Our Story" on the front. Seeing that made Samantha think about her own journey with Eli, and specifically about the night they'd watched *The Notebook* together, despite Eli's initial reservations about it being "too girly."

Eli often said that he saw a lot of Samantha in Allie Hamilton, one of the movie's lead characters. She was fiery, stubborn, and very sure of herself, which didn't always make life easy for a laidback guy like Eli. But despite how long it took for them to start a relationship and the minor tiffs they'd had along the way, dating Sam was the best thing that had ever happened to Eli. In fact, if all continued to go well, he even thought of proposing by the time graduation rolled around . . . if he could work up the nerve. But for now, Eli couldn't imagine life being much better as he twirled Sam around in *The Notebook* room. And maybe if they were lucky like Noah and Allie, their love would also last a lifetime.

*　*　*

Just lounging in the Warehouse District . . .

After the dinner dishes were neatly stacked in the dishwasher and the load of whites that had been sitting in the dryer for the past few days was folded and put away, Gavin and I were exhausted. So much for our plans to write! Our recent barrage of work had kept us apart too much lately, so we'd planned on attacking our respective projects together tonight—songwriting for him and my latest article for *Vogue*.

In addition to working on his own music, Gavin has also been writing tracks for an up-and-coming country artist, Jaguar Jones (yes, that's his real name, believe it or not). Meanwhile, I've been researching the most flattering bathing suits for summer (Really, do any exist? I'm not so sure.). But with our bellies full of pasta and our bums firmly planted on our plush, oversized couch, we decided watching TV was a far better option, as unproductive as it was. Downtime, even if it's indulging in escapist entertainment, is essential for creativity, isn't it? Gavin and I agreed that a little procrastination was perfect as we settled in with an episode of *24*.

Although *24* is one of our favorite TV shows, it's because one of our favorite pastimes is poking fun at it. Jack Bauer is a rock star and all, but far more than a simple suspension of disbelief is required to go with the flow episode after episode. No one could possibly do all that Jack does in a mere twenty-four hours—not to mention the fact that you never see him eat, sleep, or submit to any sort of authority, even if he's technically only a field agent. If that isn't enough to provide a good laugh as he saves the world from whatever nuclear disaster presents itself, some of the campy lines the screenwriters give the villains always do the trick.

But even as implausible as it all was, watching Jack Bauer in action made us feel like slackers. So after only one hour-long episode, we ventured downstairs to our small but cozy office and began our work. But just as I was about to type a headline for my swimsuit story, my cell phone rang. My caller ID revealed it was Jane.

"I ran into Campbell tonight at the singles' scavenger hunt, and he's definitely cute," Jane said breezily. "He seems a little shy, but I'm sure I could—"

"Get him to come out of his shell?" I said with a laugh. "I have no doubt you'd be able to do that. So how shall we go about getting the two of you together? Any ideas?"

"How about throwing a party at your place?" Jane offered. "That way, we could meet casually, start up a conversation, and, you know, take it from there."

"Well, it's a couple of weeks too late for Cinco de Mayo, and

Flag Day's not until next month, so what would the occasion be?"
I asked. "Oh yeah, I forgot . . . When Campbell Met Jane."

"That actually has a pretty nice ring to it, don't ya think?"
Jane asked.

"Indeed," I said. "Well, lemme talk to Gavin and see what his
schedule looks like in the next couple of weeks. Throwing a party
shouldn't be a problem at all."

"Oh, and please make it soon!" Jane said dramatically. "Did I
mention that he's really cute with his sweet little Southern accent
and all?"

"I think you already said that, but I won't hold it against you,"
I said. "I'll let you know more details as soon as I can."

After clicking off my phone, I decided that swimsuits could
wait. I had a party to plan, and I wanted to get started right away.

*　*　*

Eli starts feeling a little — okay, a lot — uneasy at Applebee's . . .

After the dance ended, Samantha's stomach was growling
something fierce. She had been having such a great time that
she'd forgotten to eat, a rarity for a three-meals-a-day stickler like
Samantha. Fortunately, salvation wasn't far away: Applebee's was
right around the corner.

Eli always thought it was funny when Samantha suggested
eating at Applebee's, considering she already waited tables there
three nights a week. But Samantha liked the appetizers and
the friendly atmosphere, not to mention the generous employee
discount. And Eli just liked being with Samantha, so he never
complained.

As it turned out, Aidan was also "eating good in the neighborhood" this particular evening. Once the hostess had seated Sam and Eli, Sam took a look around the dining room and couldn't believe her eyes. Wasn't Aidan supposed to be in India? And now he was walking right toward them. Suddenly, food didn't seem like such a good idea.

"Hi, Sam. Hi, Eli. I hoped I might find you here," Aidan said, his bright blue eyes fastened on Sam's. "I was in the mood for a burger. Thought maybe you'd be at work. I have something I picked up for you in India." He put his hand in his pocket.

"That really wasn't necessary," Samantha said a little coldly. "I thought your mission was for a year. What happened?"

"Six months," Aidan said shortly. "I'm planning on going back, but I have to sort a few things out." He pulled a small box out of his pants pocket. "Since you were the one who encouraged me to go, I wanted to—"

Before Aidan could finish his sentence, Eli nervously jumped in. "Um, Aidan, in case you didn't know, Sam and I are *dating*, and I don't appreciate you just waltzing in during *our* date so you can give *my* girlfriend a present."

Aidan turned to Eli, surprised by how flustered he was getting. Normally, Eli seemed so even-tempered. "Chill. I'm not here to steal your girl. I already ruined my chance with her—"

"Yes, you did, so why don't you do us both a favor and leave so Sam and I can enjoy the rest of the evening?" Eli said it loud enough to draw the attention of a few other patrons nearby. Heads turned.

"Sure, whatever," Aidan said and looked back at Sam. "Here, these are for you—just a small thank-you for changing my life."

Sam smiled awkwardly and tucked the box into her purse as

Aidan walked away.

Wow, she looks gorgeous. I can't believe I let her get away, he thought.

Samantha could tell Eli was angry—really angry. Even though he was dressed like Prince Charming, she knew the rest of the night wasn't going to be a fairy tale. Far from it.

"I can't believe you actually accepted a gift from him," Eli said, his cheeks growing redder by the moment. "Or have you already forgotten how much of a jerk he was when he dumped you?"

"No, I haven't forgotten," Samantha said meekly. "But there is a little thing called forgiveness. It's not like I'm holding a torch for him. Remember, I'm with you. And I've never been happier."

Eli attempted a smile. *Yes, you are with me, and I'm planning on keeping it that way*, he thought. "I guess that's why I got bent out of shape," he said. "I thought Aidan was gone for good. Seeing him again just—"

"Shhh, I know, honey," Samantha said soothingly as she rubbed Eli's shoulder. "But we don't have to worry about Aidan anymore. How about we get out of here, change out of these ridiculous clothes, and watch a movie at my place?"

"I love how you call it your place, considering your apartment is in the same building as mine," Eli said with a laugh. "That sounds wonderful."

A night in with Samantha did sound fantastic, but Eli simply couldn't escape the nagging feeling that Aidan's return would cause problems. Only time would tell, but Eli didn't like it.

CHAPTER 3

WAIT! THIS CURRY'S TOO SPICY!

You could always tell what kind of a person a man thinks you are by the earrings he gives you. I must say, the mind reels.

—HOLLY GOLIGHTLY (AUDREY HEPBURN) IN *BREAKFAST AT TIFFANY'S*, 1961

THE NEXT MORNING WHEN my alarm clock went off at eight o'clock, it nearly scared me out of bed. Gavin had left for a long day at the studio a couple of hours ago (that's six hours before most musicians even see the light of day—isn't he incredibly dedicated?), so I had our entire king-size bed to myself. Covered to my neck by our fluffy down comforter, I wanted just a few more moments of rest. But alas, there was too much to do to stay in bed any longer. Eight o'clock was actually a half hour later than I normally slept, but I'd been up way too late the night before, planning the party that would help ignite some major sparks between Jane and Campbell.

I'd decided on a chic luau theme. In the grand tradition of luaus, I'd make everyone sport a colorful lei—but the rest of the party would be sophisticated rather than kitschy. There would be no dancing hula girls, no pigs roasting on a spit, no papier-mâché flamingos. Instead, there would be candlelight, vases filled with

Hawaiian orchids and fragrant plumeria, and a menu of appetizers and desserts to die for. Oh, it was going to be so much fun! And if Jane and Campbell started dating as a result? Then mission accomplished. Wow, I *do* sound like Emma, don't I?

But now I really needed to finish up this swimsuit piece or my editor, the infamous Lucinda Buffington (who had been my boss at *Get Away*, the now-defunct travel magazine where I got my start in the writing biz) wouldn't be pleased. And saying she wouldn't be pleased is putting it mildly. She's always had a rather prickly demeanor, even though we have been getting along better than ever before. Not only is she the high-maintenance, my-nails-shall-never-be-anything-but-French-manicured type who's accustomed to everything going her way (and I mean everything, right down to the precise shade of blonde—wheat blonde—she's chosen for her hair, a color that takes her stylist a grueling half hour to mix properly), but her latest model/aspiring actor boyfriend, Martin, recently dumped her for a much younger woman (think Tom Cruise and Katie Holmes, and you'll get the picture). So Lucinda's been even more irritable than usual.

While I was always pretty sure that Martin was only using Lucinda to get into *Vogue* in the first place (hey, I'm not a cynic—just realistic), I was surprised their relationship lasted as long as it did—almost three whole months. Of course, that wasn't something I shared with Lucinda. I'm in Minneapolis, she's in Manhattan, and I didn't see their day-to-day interactions, so I tried to maintain an objective, nonjudgmental position. But when I was in New York for business a couple of months ago and went to dinner with them, Martin didn't exactly seem like the let's-settle-down-and-get-married type. He had "player" written all over his tanned, perfectly chiseled face. And if that wasn't enough of a clue about Martin's wayward intentions, he shamelessly flirted with waitress after waitress at any available moment right in front of Lucinda. Not that she noticed. She was too busy staring at his blinding white smile and bulging biceps that were in plain sight, thanks to a supertight Abercrombie T-shirt.

But when Lucinda called again and again for postbreakup support, something that surprised me because certainly she had friends who lived closer than I did, I tried to console her the best way I knew how. And because I'd heard every cliché in the book when a pre-Gavin relationship of mine went sour, I didn't tell her there were other fish in the sea or that someday her prince would come. Instead, I mostly listened and encouraged her to, perhaps, consider a relationship with someone who wasn't in the biz.

Of course, Lucinda initially thought the notion of dating a regular guy was ridiculous because she had "a reputation to maintain, being an editor at *Vogue* and all," but the last time we chatted, she mentioned that she might try finding a man at a local church.

While I liked the idea of her looking somewhere far more promising than Bungalow 8 for a date and had been praying for her to find a personal faith in Christ, this wasn't exactly the way I pictured it coming about. But then again, maybe this was another example of how God moves in mysterious ways. Who knows?

I figured I'd find out when I headed to the city soon for an assignment. But before I got too carried away thinking about New York or the upcoming luau, I decided I'd better get back to work. Sigh!

* * *

Back to class . . .

Bleary-eyed and feeling a bit nauseated from her lack of sleep last night, Samantha stumbled out of bed at 7:35 in order to make it to one of her last Marriage and Family Counseling classes. Slipping on jeans and an oversized hooded sweatshirt from her soon-to-be alma mater, one of the only clean tops in her closet at the moment, she picked up her princess outfit from last night and absently tossed it in the hamper. Then, after dotting on a little foundation, sweeping some NARS blush on her cheeks, and covering up the small blemish on her forehead, she reached down for her purse, where her Burt's Bees Beeswax was stored for her perpetually chapped lips. Noticing the small wrapped box peeking out of the top, she grew curious. *Very* curious. Although Samantha knew whatever it was wouldn't change anything between her and Aidan, she still wondered what was inside. What was so important that he actually had to interrupt her date with Eli?

After debating for another twenty seconds whether to open it or not, she ripped into the shiny gold paper with the giddiness of a three-year-old on Christmas morning. Opening the box, which Aidan had secured with what seemed like a whole roll of tape, she lifted the square of fuzzy material covering a pair of earrings that definitely weren't her taste. They were round and heavy, made out of light brown wood with pink jewel accents randomly glued on for decoration. As if to underscore how odd his choice of jewelry was for her, she also noticed the earrings were clip-on rather than pierced. *He doesn't even really know me or what I like,* she thought. *It's a good thing we're not still dating.* She crammed the box with the inferior earrings inside her desk drawer, locked the front door, and walked to class, still befuddled. *Men—seriously, what's their deal sometimes? I was right there all along, and he decides to give me a present now?*

* * *

Letting off some steam . . .

When Eli woke up bright and early for a run, as he did most days, he fully expected to be over the Aidan sighting from the night before. Without a doubt, he knew that Sam had had a great night out, and he had too. Well, until Aidan showed up. Even when they settled back into their easy camaraderie at Sam's place, where they played Scrabble until two in the morning, he'd felt unsettled. As he waited for Sam to make one of her trademark two- or three-letter words like *qi, qat,* or *xu* that resulted in beaucoup points, all he could think about was how with one unexpected gesture—a gift for *his* girlfriend—Aidan was back in Sam's life.

Eli knew he shouldn't feel threatened. His relationship with Sam had been nothing short of idyllic these past few months. He had no reason to believe that she'd ever want to get back together with Aidan, especially after he delivered what Eli considered to be one of the all-time worst lines in breakup history: "As far as women go, Samantha, you're a Ferrari . . . but sometimes what a guy really wants is a Honda." Those probably weren't his exact words, but that was the gist. He was wholeheartedly admitting that she was too good for him, and yet it was Sam who ended up feeling second-rate.

But for some reason, no matter how hard he tried, Eli couldn't run fast enough to escape the feeling that this wasn't the last time Aidan was going to come between him and his sweetie. Always the optimist, he tried to think happy thoughts. But it wasn't easy.

* * *

Swimsuits, it's a wrap! . . .

It was nearly two thirty p.m., and I was exhausted from working on the swimsuit piece for what felt like an eternity. One-pieces, tankinis, bikinis in every cut and color under the sun, and I'd written about the latest designs of each and every one for *Vogue*'s comprehensive guide. Well, except for the thong bottoms. I mean really, what was the point? It seemed like a crime that any designer would charge $150 for such a small swathe of uncomfortable material.

But it all wrapped up rather nicely (no pun intended), so now I was heading over to India Palace, a quaint little bistro not far from Bethel University. I was meeting Samantha for a late lunch. She was done with classes for the day, and it had been ages since I'd seen her (busy schedules and cute boys in your life will do that!), so I was really looking forward to catching up.

* * *

Meanwhile, back at the office . . .

As Aidan crunched the numbers at his old desk at Wells Fargo Mortgage, something he could still do in his sleep despite having been away for the past few months, he couldn't stop thinking about how conflicted he felt about seeing Samantha again. Not only did he feel his heartstrings tug when he saw how beautiful she looked, but her glowing face also reminded him of his many shortcomings. She'd been the one who inspired him to go to India in the first place, and he'd felt like such a failure ever since he'd gotten back to Minnesota.

Initially, he felt like he'd returned from India a changed man. Seeing all that he did—beggars on every street corner, the sad but still hopeful children sleeping on the floor at the orphanage he visited each day—Aidan felt like he was doing what he was born to do when he was ministering there. He was never more content than when he was kicking a soccer ball or coloring with the kids. Their bright smiles always warmed his heart. Yet when he'd reached the end of his commitment and had to make a decision to stay or return, the temptations of comfortable American living were too much. The kids' smiles were easily forgotten in favor of the multitude of luxuries he was missing.

He longed for his plush, queen-size bed. A hot shower. A steaming hot mocha from Starbucks. It surprised him how easy it was to adapt back to his old life. Although Aidan had happily left his six-figure job behind, he found its invisible clutches impossible to resist when he'd contacted his boss to see if there was still a place for him at Wells Fargo. "Absolutely, Aidan," his boss had replied without a hint of hesitation. And before he knew it, Aidan found his thoughts wandering into uncomfortable territory as he wondered what Sam thought of the earrings he'd bought her. Or what it would be like to kiss her again. And the worst? How he could steal her from Eli.

Before he entertained that notion any longer, though, he needed sustenance. So he decided to head to the closest Indian restaurant, a deliberate decision he hoped would remind him of his purpose and why he went to India in the first place.

❋ ❋ ❋

Time for a little girl talk . . .

No matter how much time passes between visits, it never takes long for Samantha and I to pick right up where we've left off. Over bowls of spicy red curry and flaky naan, Samantha and I talked way more than we ate. If only all lunches could be virtually calorie-free like this!

After catching up on what was new with Gavin and me, Samantha told me she could hardly believe that graduation was just around the corner. She also mentioned that she hadn't quite figured out what her next career step would be, something our mom had been nagging her about incessantly.

"Seriously, she's calling at least every other day now," Samantha said with a sigh. "Like I don't have enough pressure already."

"The same thing happened to me when everything wasn't coming together immediately after I graduated," I said sympathetically. "I guess that's what moms do best—they worry."

"I guess so," Samantha said, before adding in her best mock valley girl voice, "It's majorly annoying."

Samantha has managed to narrow her career options down to two. Currently, she's deciding between grad school at the University of Minnesota (so she can work toward becoming a marriage and family counselor) or pursuing full-time missions for a year or two before heading back to school.

There are pros and cons to both scenarios, of course, so we immediately started weighing those. Deep in thought, we barely noticed anyone around us, let alone who walked in and out of the restaurant. Too bad.

As I reached for my purse to find something to write our pros and cons list down on, I noticed Aidan inching closer to our table. *Aidan!* I couldn't even warn Sam because he was already way too close.

"Hey, Sam, I've been seeing a lot of you lately," Aidan said with a mischievous smile. Then turning my way, he said hello, while I unsuccessfully tried to hide my feeling of sheer disgust.

"Aren't you supposed to be in India?"

"What, Sam didn't tell you? My commitment was up. Now I have to decide if I'm going back." He smiled. "I've really been missing the food."

"By all means, don't let us stop you," I replied, my tone probably more snide than it needed to be.

Ignoring me, Aidan turned to Samantha and asked if he could sit down. It was all I could do to keep my mouth shut. *The nerve of him! Doesn't he know that Sam is dating Eli? Seriously, what is this guy's problem? Can't he take a hint? Sit down? That's sooo not happening.*

Glancing at me hesitantly, Samantha said, "Sure," and Aidan didn't waste any time settling in.

"So, Sydney, how's married life?" he asked. "I saw a pic of you and your hubby on MySpace. You two look really happy."

"We *are* really happy," I replied flatly, not offering any more information than necessary. "So how about you, Aidan? Meet any — oh, what was it — *Hondas* lately?"

Sam nearly choked on a coriander seed in her red curry. "Sydney!"

"No, she's well within her right to say that," Aidan said. "That was probably the lamest—and rudest—comment I ever made to a girl, let alone one I really cared about. I guess I hoped the earrings would be a peace offering."

Earrings? I looked at Samantha, annoyed. When had she been planning to tell me this? Sam just shrugged.

"You know, you just don't go around giving earrings to someone who is dating someone else!" I said. "If you ask me, you're no less selfish now than you were before."

"Good thing I wasn't asking," Aidan said, then stood up. "I've had enough. I guess it was a mistake, thinking I could share a meal with an old friend." And with no further adieu, he took one last look at Samantha and walked away.

"I hope you're happy, Syd," Samantha said quietly. "There was no reason to act like that."

"There was no reason for him to sit down!" I said, my voice growing loud enough for other customers to start looking our way. "You could've told him to take a hike."

Embarrassed by my volume, Sam said, "Let's get out of here and talk about this somewhere else. I'm tired of being everyone's entertainment."

"Fair enough," I said mildly, collecting my things. Sisters are quick to forgive. "Want to head over to your place?"

"Yeah, that's probably better," Sam said. "A little less commotion."

CHAPTER 4

OPEN MOUTH, INSERT FOOT!

I think that, a) you have an act, and that, b) not having an
act is your act.

—LINDA POWELL (KYRA SEDGWICK) IN *SINGLES*, 1992

A S SAMANTHA DROVE THE ten or so minutes to her on-campus
apartment, she was replaying the ill-fated lunch in her mind.
Why did Aidan have to show up? And when he did, why did
Sydney have to be so, well, combative? She had just made it all
worse somehow.

What was even more confusing for Samantha was the conflict-
ing feelings she'd been dealing with ever since Aidan had showed
up at Applebee's. As much as she loved Eli, there was something
about Aidan that still intrigued her. No matter how hard she tried,
she couldn't seem to get him off her mind. Maybe it was because he
was finally living out his life's calling in India. She hoped it wasn't
just those piercing blue eyes that had gotten the best of her before.
Whatever it was, Samantha was seriously questioning her mental
state at the moment. With something so special with Eli, why was
she even thinking of Aidan? It just didn't make sense.

* * *

A call to Gavin to calm me down . . .

Even though it was a short drive to Sam's place, I needed some clarity after our crazy lunch, so I pulled over and called my sweet, long-suffering husband. Growing up with two sisters, he was accustomed to the dramas that inevitably happen when girls get together, so I knew he'd understand.

"Hey, baby, how's your day going?"

"It's been great—very productive," Gavin said. "I helped Jaguar finish up two songs and have been working on that one song I was telling you about."

"Oh, the mysterious one that you won't let me hear?"

"The very one," Gavin replied. "You'll hear it soon enough. How's Sam?"

"Interesting, to say the least. Aidan ended up showing up out of the blue and decided to make himself at home by sitting with us. I was not happy, and well, I got a little rude—"

"What do you mean you got a little *rude*?" Gavin asked, laughing. He knew Aidan wasn't my favorite person, but he always thought the best of me. Which made me a better person.

"I made some pretty sarcastic comments about his behavior. He ended up leaving in a huff."

"Sounds like you were honest in the moment," Gavin said reassuringly. "There's nothing wrong with that."

"Have I told you lately that I love you so much?" I asked, so thankful for an amazing man who always listens, even when I make a fool out of myself.

"I love to hear it," Gavin said. "Love ya too. Hope things go better with Sam."

"Thanks, baby. I'll see ya for a late dinner?"

"Maybe eightish."

And when I snapped my phone shut, I felt so much better. Husbands just have a way of doing that.

* * *

While she was waiting for me to show up, Samantha set up some tea and homemade scones on the kitchen table. These little touches were a reminder of her time spent in Europe.

"It's about time you got here," she said in mock seriousness as she opened the door and welcomed me inside. "I thought you'd forgotten where I live."

"Nah, I was talking to Gavin—basically telling him what a complete idiot I was this afternoon," I said. "I really do feel bad for snapping at Aidan. But someone has to tell the guy when he's being selfish. In retrospect, maybe I wasn't the right person. I hardly know the guy."

"That's true," Sam said as she slathered her scone with blackberry jam. "You mostly know him by the stories I've told you."

"I know. But I've never really liked the guy, never trusted him, even when you were dating. There was just something too slick about him. He always sort of struck me as the used-car-salesman type."

"You never saw how he was with me, though, Syd," Samantha said, her eyes looking wistful. "I didn't just like him because he's good-looking. He's got such amazing potential. He—"

"It's Florence Nightingale syndrome. Didn't get me far with Daniel, Justin, Liam—"

"Ah, Liam, that's a name I haven't heard in a while," Sam said with a laugh. "Thank goodness Gavin came to your rescue."

"Thank goodness indeed, but you're changing the subject," I said, my tone turning serious. "I'm a little worried about you. It sounds like you're still carrying a torch for Aidan."

Samantha took a couple of seconds to collect her thoughts, knowing it wouldn't be easy to explain her feelings. "It's complicated. My emotions have been all jumbled since he showed up," she said softly. "I have this incredible relationship with Eli — he's my best friend, and I've loved every moment we've spent together. Yet for some reason, all I can think about is Aidan, and I wonder if things would be different this time. Something's seriously wrong with me, isn't it?"

"Maybe you're trying to sabotage your own happiness," I offered. "Eli would never treat you the way Aidan has. Aidan doesn't even respect your relationship with Eli enough to leave you alone."

"I know," Samantha began. "But why can't I stop thinking about him?"

"I don't know. Probably the same reason I couldn't stop thinking about Liam, even though I got duped again and again. Seriously, you don't want to go through that."

"You're right, I need to be sensible," Samantha said. "Sensible it is. I've got a great thing with Eli, and I'm not going to let Aidan ruin that."

"I'm glad to hear that, Sam," I said, not entirely believing that's what she really wanted.

✳ ✳ ✳

It's singles' group night at Jane's . . .

Across town in her Victorian-style abode, Jane was carefully arranging a colorful spread of homemade chocolate cupcakes with sprinkles on her dining room table for tonight's Bible study. Normally, she didn't host the weekly festivities, but when one of the group's coleaders came down with the flu, Jane happily stepped in. Even if leading a Bible study wasn't really her thing.

Jane had many of the qualities that befitted someone with such a no-nonsense name. Tonight she'd be the first to admit she had an ulterior motive for opening up her home, since she generally preferred to be in the background. Still, she hoped Campbell would show up.

Ever since Sydney had mentioned Campbell as a potential dating possibility, Jane was intrigued. She never would've thought of it on her own; the singles' pastor seemed off-limits somehow. But after she and Campbell had shared a few conversations—albeit brief ones—Jane quickly realized there was so much to like about Campbell. In her humble opinion (and Jane was known for not being particularly shy about sharing her two cents on anything), he had that perfect mix of wit and intelligence. And from the pulpit, Campbell never came across as pompous or fake, two qualities that Jane detested about most preachers. Instead of trying to impress everyone with his highbrow seminary education, Campbell's messages always had practical takeaway value and thoughtful insight. Definitely an attractive quality.

As if she needed yet another reason to crush on the singles' pastor, it also didn't hurt that he was boyishly cute, a quality that manifested itself the most whenever he smiled. Like her last serious boyfriend, the illustrious (or so he thought) weekend anchorman

Perry Woodhouse, Campbell had a deep-set dimple on the right side of his face and an ever-so-slight space between his otherwise perfect white teeth. What would technically be considered imperfections gave each of them a look that said, *I'm down-to-earth; you can trust me.* Of course, in Perry's case, his adorable dimple eventually wasn't enough to redeem him from a host of flaws, like forgetting her birthday or failing to mention that he'd been engaged not once, but twice, something Jane found out only when one of the jilted brides-to-be turned up at a mutual friend's baby shower. Funny thing was that she and Harriet (otherwise known as fiancée number two) ended up becoming great friends after Jane and Perry called it quits. Lose a significant other, gain a new friend. If only all relationships worked that way.

Aside from that sizeable list of complaints, however, the worst problem with Perry was that he didn't want someone competing with him for the spotlight at work. No matter how many great news stories Jane wrote and delivered on-air, Perry preferred his girlfriends to be a little less visible. And he dropped hints about this several times without coming right out and saying it.

In fact, when Jane was promoted to anchor, something Perry fully expected with Jane's camera-ready good looks and credible reporting, he'd found it difficult to be genuinely happy for her. When Jane had suggested celebrating this career milestone, Perry kept making excuses for why he couldn't get together before finally agreeing to—two weeks after the fact. Later on, Perry hated it even more when locals would recognize Jane on the street. The final straw was when a random guy asked Jane for an autograph during dinner. Perry was the one with celebrity aspirations—not Jane—and he didn't like any girl, let alone his girlfriend, stealing his thunder. So they'd agreed to start seeing other people.

But then something weird happened. After Perry, guys just stopped asking Jane out altogether. Countless times Jane's friends had told her it was because guys probably thought they were out of her league. Jane didn't get it; she hadn't changed. She was sure it was some mysterious please-don't-ask-me-out vibe she was giving off. But after such a long spell without a date, save the setup with Weston, Jane was feeling, well, desperate.

But Campbell, sweet Campbell . . . He didn't seem like the type who'd be intimidated by her success. Now if she could only get to know him better — which was exactly what Jane hoped to do tonight, a few nights before she'd see him again at Sydney's luau. She could hardly contain her excitement!

*　*　*

Sweatin' to the oldies . . .

After hanging out with Sydney, Samantha started to feel better about the Aidan debacle. On the way to the gym, she'd come to the realization that Aidan was like one of those fruit tarts in the fancy baking cases of upscale restaurants. On the outside, it was the picture of perfection. But somehow, once you actually got down to tasting the pastry, it definitely wasn't worth all the calories. Not even close. It looked far better than it actually was.

So with her resolve firmly in place, Samantha clicked on her iPod and listened to some vintage Led Zeppelin tracks as she power-walked on the treadmill. But then just as "Heartbreaker" blared, she spotted someone who looked like Aidan, and the whole crazy cycle started all over again. Like the Alcoholics

Anonymous member who calls her sponsor the moment before she orders that vodka tonic and falls off the wagon, Samantha immediately stopped the treadmill, toweled off, picked up her cell phone, and texted Sydney.

✳ ✳ ✳

Oh, the thrill of anticipation . . .

Just before praise and worship started, Jane excused herself so she could reapply her lip gloss in the bathroom. If Campbell was going to be there, she wanted to look her best, and MAC's Viva Glam usually did the trick. As she looked in the mirror and began applying the sticky gloss to her lips, she suddenly felt a little self-conscious. Jane hadn't put this much effort into her appearance since Perry—let alone for someone she didn't know. *Oh good grief,* she thought. *It's only a little lip gloss.*

A psychologist would say Jane had trust issues—and rightly so. Perry hadn't been kind to her self-esteem. But once Jane crossed the threshold from the girl who happily stayed home and knitted on Friday nights to the girl who was willing to embrace new dating opportunities (even sketchy ones like her recent night out with Weston), she began to feel like herself again, which made her feel incredible and alive.

Then as Jane walked out to the living room and took her seat, she immediately noticed Campbell, hands raised in worship, across the room. And when they locked eyes as they sang a simple praise chorus, Jane's heart started beating faster, causing her to hope yet again that Sydney had been right about him.

✳ ✳ ✳

48

Heading over to the studio . . .

After we grabbed a quick Tex-Mex dinner, Gavin surprised me by taking me to his makeshift studio, some cheap storage space a few blocks from home that he'd converted into a soundproof place to practice. "I have something to play for you," he said as he opened the car for me. "It's finally ready."

"You mean *the* song?" I asked as I fished my cell phone out of my purse to see who had texted me. "I can't wait to hear it, baby!"

He grinned. "Who texted you, anyway?"

Although the three little words looked innocent enough on the phone's tiny screen, the capital letters seemed ominous somehow. CALL ME NOW.

"It's Sam. She wants me to call her. Now. I guess it's some sort of emergency."

"An actual emergency? Or like the time she took those green tea diet pills and thought she was having a heart attack?" Gavin said with a laugh. "Better call her back and see."

"All right. Hopefully it'll just take a minute," I said as I dialed.

"Don't worry about it," Gavin said. "I'll warm up while you chat. Want to get the song just right."

"Ah, there's the perfectionist husband I love. I'm sure it'll only take a minute."

* * *

Just killin' time . . .

Of course, Gavin knew it wouldn't only be a minute. Or ten. This was Sydney and Samantha talking, and it was rare for them to talk less than, oh, twenty minutes. In the meantime, Gavin would have plenty of time to change his guitar strings (like food, fresh was always better), get his beloved Martin in tune, and practice his new favorite song.

❋　❋　❋

Breathe in, breathe out . . .

Sam let her phone ring three times before she answered. She had to regain her composure so Sydney wouldn't worry too much. Even though Sydney was the coolest sister a girl could ask for, she was also the oldest, making her a natural worrywart.

"So what's up, girl? Your message had me a little worried," her sister said. "Is it Mom? Eli—"

"No, it's me, actually. I'm fine, it's just this whole Aidan thing."

Sydney sighed, and Sam could hear what she wasn't saying: After their entire conversation this afternoon, they were back at square one.

"Did you run into him again?" Sydney asked.

"No, but I saw someone who looked just like him at the gym, and I panicked," Samantha said. "I started freaking out, so I had to leave and call you."

"*That* was the emergency—an Aidan look-alike?" Syd sputtered. "Haven't we been through this already? I thought someone had died. Or was seriously ill."

"I know, I know. But I thought you'd be able to empathize after everything you went through with Liam. We all told you he was a mistake, but you kept holding on," Samantha replied.

Sydney paused, and Samantha could tell she'd hit home with that.

"But the difference was that I didn't already have an amazing boyfriend," Sydney said defensively. "I was holding on to something that clearly wasn't meant to be. You can't really love Eli all that much if you still can't get Aidan off your mind."

And then, a brainstorm: "Maybe you should just break up with Eli and give it another try with Aidan if that's what you really want."

After several seconds of silence with the words *break up with Eli* still in the air, Samantha said, "Maybe you're right. Thanks, Syd, this has been helpful."

"You're welcome, Sam. Love ya."

"Love you too."

And after Samantha hung up with Sydney, she knew exactly what she had to do.

✼　✼　✼

Back at the studio . . .

"Well, I do believe you were gone for more than a minute," Gavin said as he walked over and planted a kiss on my lips.

"Yeah, relationship drama—it's never easy," I said. "Now, how about that song?"

Gavin had constructed a makeshift stage in the cramped

studio quarters, and now he picked up the microphone. In his best radio announcer voice, he said to the pretend crowd of thousands, "I'd like to dedicate this song to my beautiful wife, Sydney. It's called 'Star-Crossed Puppy Love.'"

And then he began to sing the most beautiful song to his audience of one.

> I want breakfast with you in the morning
> with Cupid, milk, and honey dribbling down our
>   chins
> as we laugh at something stupid.
> I want to dance with you in the morning.
> Roses are red.
> You're an angel with bed head.

The song was definitely worth the wait. And then some . . .

CHAPTER 5

NO MORE MR. NICE GUY

Did he dazzle you with his extensive knowledge of mineral water? Or was it his in-depth analysis of, uh, uh, Marky Mark that finally reeled you in?

— TROY DYER (ETHAN HAWKE) IN *REALITY BITES*, 1994

IT TOOK SAMANTHA THREE days to work up the courage to get in touch with Aidan. She'd deleted Aidan's number from her cell phone several months ago, so she wasn't able to call him. She had also erased his e-mail address (and loads of messages he'd sent her while they dated), so writing him was officially out too. The only way she knew to find him was to go to the gym. Before he'd gone to India, he'd lifted weights every other day without fail at the Lifetime Fitness near Bethel University, always starting at seven p.m. He'd probably resumed that habit. Samantha hadn't worked out exactly what she planned to say, but she'd decided to stop by and "casually" run into him. The rest she'd play by ear.

Samantha also knew a talk with Eli would be in order, something she dreaded. She knew Eli wouldn't be happy (the understatement of the century) about taking a break, whether or not she mentioned Aidan. But as much as Samantha tried to convince herself that Aidan didn't matter to her, she couldn't. And that wasn't fair to Eli.

So after changing her shirt and smoothing her hair just enough to look pretty without putting much effort into it, Samantha made her way to Lifetime Fitness to face her relationship crisis head-on.

✻ ✻ ✻

The mood is festive at Gavin and Syd's place . . .

It was a few minutes after seven thirty, and guests were steadily trickling in to the luau party. I thought the mix of chic and novelty decorations was working really well. And everyone was mingling and nibbling away on appetizers — always a good sign. The secret guests of honor were already here, and I was plotting the best time to bring them together.

Oh, I couldn't wait any longer.

I tapped Jane on the shoulder and gave her the signal (nothing 007-ish, just a nudge to let her know the play was imminent). As usual, Jane looked flawless in a white bohemian-style blouse, chunky brown beads, a distressed knee-length denim skirt, and tall brown boots. And I was going to make sure Campbell knew that she's also incredibly smart, talented, and sweet. How could he not want to go out with her?

"Campbell," I said, "have you met Jane yet? I think she wants to talk to you for one of her stories for KARE-11."

Sure, it was a little white lie, but it got the conversation going.

And even though it wasn't Jane's intention to talk shop with

Campbell, my plan worked. The singles' pastor and the prettiest girl in the singles' group were talking up a storm.

❋   ❋   ❋

A creature of habit gets the surprise of his life . . .

Even though his muscles still ached terribly—he was out of shape from not lifting for so long—Aidan loved feeling the burn from working out. It left him with a tangible sense of accomplishment, not to mention much buffer biceps that always won him approval from the ladies. And thinking about the ladies naturally made him think of Sam. Aidan wasn't usually the introspective type who ruminated on the past, but as he finished a set of leg presses, Aidan found himself wishing he could travel back in time. Right the wrongs. Enjoy what he and Sam had before he so carelessly threw it away. And for what? Fear of actually having a future together? Sheesh.

Then as Aidan stood up to add more weight to the machine, he saw Sam walking toward him. Was he seeing things? Delusional? Could that really be Samantha? Could he really be that lucky?

"Hi, Aidan," Samantha said, grinning like a girl with a juicy secret. "Didn't expect to see me, huh?"

"What was your first clue?"

"Oh, I don't know, you've got that deer-in-the-headlights thing going on," Samantha said.

"Sorry, uh, hmmm, I—"

"I know, it was rude of me to drop in like this, but I had to see you," Samantha said. "There's so much that's unresolved between us. At least for me."

"What about Eli?" Aidan asked. "Aren't you two dating?"

"We are, but I'm not sure that's what I want right now," Sam said. Then without hesitating, she added, "Seeing you again made me realize that I still have feelings for you."

And then Aidan's face turned almost as white as Minnesota snow. At first Samantha thought it was what she'd said, the way she'd put her feelings right out there. Seconds later, Samantha realized it wasn't *what* she said that mattered, but *who* was within earshot as she bared her soul.

Turns out Eli was also in the mood to pump iron that evening.

✷ ✷ ✷

Flirting the night away . . .

Maybe it was the way Campbell asked Jane if she was "fixin' to go to the upcoming singles' barbeque." Or perhaps it was the whiff of cologne (Allure, which had also been Perry's favorite) she got when Campbell leaned in to show her the scratch he got from wrestling with his golden retriever puppy, Ginger, the other day. But whatever it was, Campbell was proving to be even more promising than Jane imagined. She'd definitely have to thank Sydney for arranging such a fabulous official meeting.

And if all continued to go well, Jane was confident she'd have a date by the end of the evening. Fingers crossed, anyway.

✷ ✷ ✷

The gym's never been sweatier . . .

Samantha had never felt more sick to her stomach than she did right then. And to add insult to injury, she was sweating something fierce. Eli, her *boyfriend* Eli, heard every word she said, and now he had a look on his face that she'd never seen before. His eyes were fiery and determined, and his cheeks flushed a sunburned shade of red. Clearly Eli was angry, and it looked like he was prepared to do something about it, which was so out of character for a cuddly, fun-loving guy like him.

It was like she was watching a movie in slow motion. With a stalwart sense of determination and a quick flick of his wrist, Eli did something he'd dreamed about doing countless times before. He punched Aidan square in the nose, took one last look at Sam, and simply walked away.

Blood dripping from his nose, Aidan was in a state of shock. "I can't believe he actually punched me," he said as Sam handed him tissues from her purse. "It was like he planned it."

"Well, he's probably thought about it before," Sam said, pacing back and forth nervously. "I'm sure what I said didn't help matters much. I'm so sorry."

"You've got nothing to be sorry about," Aidan said reassuringly as he continued to dab his nose. "Want to go somewhere to talk?"

"Yeah, I think talking would be good," Sam said, her stomach feeling more nauseated by the moment. "You name the time and place, and I'm there."

* * *

Retreating to his rusty Volkswagon . . .

In retrospect, punching Aidan had played out a lot better in his head than it did in real time. Not only did Eli's hand still hurt from giving Aidan a good wallop, but so did his wounded pride. When it came down to it, what he really wanted—Sam's love—was gone. Possibly for good.

How can she still care about him? Eli thought as tears streamed down his face. *Didn't we have a really good thing going? Or was that all a façade? And why would she want something with Aidan, the guy who made her feel like crap? What's wrong with me?* Somehow he'd known something bad was going to happen, but deep down he'd hoped it wouldn't.

The more Eli sat there trying to figure it all out, the less it made sense. So he stuck his key in the ignition, cranked up the classic rock station, and drove from Roseville to Lake Calhoun to clear his head. Or at least to give it his best effort.

* * *

Saying aloha for the evening . . .

Around nine thirty, Jane was helping me clean up after the luau. "I'd say our plotting went pretty well for you and Campbell," I said to Jane as I wiped off the countertops and put the leftover food away. "You were gabbing away."

"We had a great conversation," Jane said. "I felt like I really got to know him. But I was a little disappointed that he didn't ask for my number or anything. We flirted all night, and then . . . nothing."

"Well, he's got to be discreet," I began. "He is the singles' pastor, so he has a lot to consider, especially if he starts dating someone from the group."

"Yeah, I guess you're right. I'm antsy, that's all," Jane replied as she took over cleaning the counters. "I guess my self-confidence is still a little low."

"But that's all behind you, honey," I offered. "I think tonight was a promising step in a new direction. You have to be patient. Campbell will be worth the wait."

"You're right. I'm just not very good at waiting," Jane said. "But I really don't have any other choice, right?"

* * *

Starting over at Caribou Coffee . . .

Aidan and Samantha had agreed to meet at a nearby Caribou Coffee. Aidan arrived about ten minutes after Samantha did, so she'd already reserved a corner table. The shop was only open for another hour, but that was plenty of time to start figuring out what exactly was going on. For Samantha, it was surreal to return to the place where she and Aidan had shared so many meaningful conversations—and nonfat white chocolate mochas—in the past. But even more shocking was that she'd ended things with Eli to see if Aidan was right for her. It was like betting on a team with fifty-to-one odds. It definitely wasn't what Samantha would normally do. She was much too practical for that. Yet as much as it hurt her to think how Eli must be feeling right now, it was a relief not to be having this conversation with Aidan behind Eli's back. Having it all out in the open liberated Samantha somehow—like she could have a real shot with Aidan.

Samantha's heart pounded wildly like it had on their first date as soon as she saw Aidan walking toward her. "Still drinking nonfat white mochas, Sam?" Aidan asked as he fidgeted with a handmade bracelet on his arm that Sam hadn't noticed before.

"Yeah, but I'd better have decaf at this hour. I've actually got quite a bit of studying to do this weekend."

"Decaf it is. I'll be right back," Aidan said. "Don't try to sneak off or something while I'm gone."

That thought had crossed Samantha's mind a time or two. But that was the fear talking. Deep down, she knew anything worth pursuing involved risk. And she'd already taken the biggest leap of faith by telling Aidan how she felt, so this was the easy part.

Aidan returned a couple of minutes later, mochas in hand.

"Thanks," Samantha said shyly. "So is it just me or does this feel, well—"

"Yeah, it's a little weird. But in a way, it's not," Aidan said. "I've missed hanging out with you, Sam. Not being able to tell you about India hasn't felt right. Believe it or not, that experience changed me. So much is different now."

"I'm glad to hear that," Samantha said. "But I do have a question."

"Shoot."

"If you've been so excited about what's happening there and you plan to return, why are you trying to, you know, patch things up with me?" Samantha asked. "Long-distance relationships are hard enough when someone lives in another state, let alone on another continent."

"I know," Aidan said sympathetically. "I haven't exactly worked it all out yet. It's not like I was expecting you to show up at the gym tonight. You were dating Eli, remember?"

Ouch, that stung. A zingy retort was in order—and fast. "That didn't exactly stop you from saying hi at Applebee's, did it?" Samantha said with a hint of sarcasm. "But you're right: I can't expect you to have it all figured out—"

"But it's something I *want* to figure out," Aidan said. "I need time to mull things over and pray. Does that sound good?"

"It does," Samantha said confidently. "It really does."

Moments before Caribou Coffee was about to close its doors, Aidan walked Samantha to her car, gave her a quick hug, and said good night.

And as nice as that was, Samantha really couldn't believe that she and Aidan were starting over.

* * *

Heading back on 35W . . .

After walking about halfway around Lake Calhoun in the almost-dark, Eli wasn't feeling much better. His feelings morphed from sadness to anger and back to sadness as he looked at the starry sky and prayed. *God, I don't understand why this is happening. Why did Samantha turn on me like this? Did she ever really love me? I'm so confused, God, and I need you now. Please be with me.*

Though Eli's soul felt a little better after he spilled his guts to God, his flesh was still weak. Whenever Aidan's face popped into his head, he wanted to punch something. After he took his anger out on a large pine tree and lost (truth be told, his hand felt broken), Eli decided it was time to leave. When he opened his car door and saw his cell phone on the seat, he considered calling Samantha to find out exactly why she wanted to pursue something with Aidan. But after dialing six of the seven numbers that would connect them, he hung up. He couldn't bear to hear her voice. Not now anyway. Making amends wasn't going to be easy.

✻ ✻ ✻

After Samantha got back to her place, she gave Eli a call. The phone rang three times, and just before Samantha was sure the call was going to voice mail, Eli picked up.

"Hello?" he offered weakly, his voice still a little scratchy from crying.

"Hi. It's me," Samantha said as she nervously picked at her cuticles. "But hey, you've got caller ID. So you knew."

"Yeah," Eli said. "I considered not answering, but I might as well face the inevitable, huh?"

"Eli, I'm so sorry. I never meant to hurt you. It's just—"

"You never meant to hurt me, I believe that," Eli said, pacing back and forth in his apartment. "But you sure didn't think much of our relationship. Apparently Aidan's got something I don't."

Samantha paused and carefully chose her next words. "Eli, I really do care about you. I know I have a pretty funny way of showing that right now. But I guess I—"

And before Samantha could fill in the blank, Eli hung up. He was far too hurt to hear the end of her explanation. Whatever it was, he wasn't going to feel better hearing it, and with one *click*, he didn't have to.

CHAPTER 6

MANOLOS AND MAYHEM

By all means move at a glacial pace. You know how that thrills me.

—MIRANDA PRIESTLY (MERYL STREEP) IN *THE DEVIL WEARS PRADA*, 2006

BEFORE SAMANTHA KNEW IT, it was Monday. A rainy Monday no less, the sort of morning where she'd much prefer to camp out on her ugly orange couch with her favorite blanket and a cup of coffee as she flipped channels all day. But this leisurely pipe dream definitely wasn't an option today. It was finals week, her last finals week of her college career, and Samantha couldn't help but feel a little wistful.

I can't believe this is really it. I won't be coming back to Bethel next year; I'll actually be a college grad. A grown-up. What will life be like? What will I do next? There were still so many unanswered questions.

The weekend had passed much too quickly for Samantha's comfort, even though it was incredibly productive. She'd diligently studied for all of her psych classes, even when focusing wasn't particularly easy, what with all the new developments in her dating life. Just days ago, she and Eli had talked about what an amazing summer they were going to have together. And now

Eli wasn't even a part of her life; Aidan was. Aidan who hadn't even bothered to call her since they'd met up for coffee Friday night.

What was it with guys and the phone lately? First Eli hung up on her, and then Aidan didn't seem to know how to pick one up.

Samantha wanted to think she was cooler—and more laid-back—about everything with Aidan this time around. But she was just as nervous, maybe even *more* nervous, because she'd sacrificed what she had with Eli to explore the unknown with Aidan. Samantha definitely felt like she'd made the right decision, but when her phone continued *not* to ring, she worried. Had his affections already waned? She sure hoped not.

As much as Samantha wanted to mull all of that over, she had to get to class—and fast. After all, now was not the time for slacking. Samantha wanted to keep a respectable GPA so she'd have plenty of scholarship opportunities available if she did end up pursuing grad school. So many options . . .

❀ ❀ ❀

It's just another manic Monday in Manhattan . . .

After saying good-bye to Gavin at the Minneapolis/St. Paul airport yesterday afternoon (it was the first time we'd been apart—overnight, anyway—since we'd been married, and I was missing him already), I made my way to the Big Apple for a writing assignment for Lucinda.

Of course it's never *just* a writing assignment with Lucinda. She needed me to do her a favor—a big favor that she promised she'd elaborate on more at lunch today.

I'd been in New York City for less than twenty-four hours, and it was already a crazy trip. I guess I probably should've known better, though. Crazy's just par for the course whenever Lucinda is involved. But despite our prickly relationship at *Get Away*, Lucinda and I are practically BFFs now, thanks to how many times I've bailed her out since she came to *Vogue*. Lucinda even insists I stay with her when I come to town, which definitely helps financially.

But progress aside, that doesn't mean I don't still get annoyed with her demanding personality. Basically, since my plane touched down, I'd been running around nonstop. So much so that my feet already had blisters from walking so much. The blisters were technically my own fault, though: I really knew better than to wear my uncomfortable tall black leather boots for more than a few blocks. But as painful as they were to squish my feet into, they just went so much better with my outfit than my UGGs. You understand, right? When in New York, fashion always trumps function.

To make matters even more interesting, sleeping in apparently wasn't in the cards either. Lucinda's alarm clock went off at five forty-five this morning, giving her time to properly "put her face on." Her words, not mine, just for the record. As she rubbed her pricey La Mer face cream into her high cheekbones and expertly lined her lips with a satiny shade of Chanel, I ventured out a couple of blocks for a real New York bagel with cream cheese. Although I'm happy with a Panera bagel back home, there's just something superior about the NYC brand of carbs. They're perfectly chewy on the inside and crisp on the outside — basically worth every empty calorie.

As I patiently waited for the next batch to come out of the

oven, I accidentally made eye contact with the guy standing next to me who'd just placed a huge bagel order—one hundred in all. Instead of turning his glance away like the stereotypical New Yorker, he made small talk. Looking at me, he asked, "So what kind are you waiting for?"

"Honey wheat," I replied without much thought. "You?"

"I'm an everything bagel guy myself," he said. "It's got all four major food groups: poppy seeds, sesame seeds, garlic, salt—"

"Nothing like a well-balanced diet," I joked. I was surprised to find that I was comfortable having this conversation with an attractive man. I wasn't being unfaithful to Gavin; in fact, my marriage to him gave me the freedom to enjoy this guy's company, knowing that in five minutes we'd go our separate ways.

"So I have to ask, are you stocking up on bagels today? You must have ordered at least fifteen different kinds." I knew it really wasn't any of my business. But if small talk meant I'd get my bagel faster, I was game.

"They're actually for my men's Bible study group," Mystery Guy said. "We meet before work a couple of times a week, and it's my turn to bring the bagels."

"You have that many guys in your Bible study group?" I asked. "On a good night my women's Bible study has twenty. Or wait a minute . . . maybe there's just a few guys who *really* like bagels."

"We do like our bagels," Mystery Guy said with an easy laugh. "We actually have a few homeless men who join us each week, though. It may be just for the free bagels, but I'd like to think they're craving the spiritual sustenance too."

"That's incredible," I said with a smile. "Any converts recently?"

"Two just last week," he offered proudly. "It's been exciting to see the changes in their lives."

"Wow," I said. "That's very cool."

Then, noticing he wasn't wearing a wedding band, I thought about Lucinda. A seemingly great Christian guy who helps the homeless in New York City would be a vast improvement over the latest model/actor she dated, right? So I did something I'd never done before.

"I know this may seem a little strange in a bagel shop and all, but . . . are you married?" I asked Mystery Guy.

"Are you considering polygamy or just hoping to set me up with one of your friends?" he quipped.

He probably gets set up a lot, I thought to myself. He was nicely dressed, articulate, funny.

"Okay, you got me," I said, laughing at his quick wit. "I was playing Cupid. Or attempting to."

"What's she like?"

Not having planned my proposition, I ad-libbed. *What to say about Lucinda? . . . What to say about Lucinda that won't scare him off before he even meets her?*

"Lucinda is my editor at *Vogue*," I began. "She's smart, funny, and driven, and for some reason, she only seems to date guys who have the intelligence of a common housefly."

"Why do you think that happens?" Mystery Guy asked.

Maybe because she's superficial. Maybe because she favors vapid men over quality ones. Maybe . . . Shoot, my mind was wandering again.

"You know, I think it's because she doesn't believe that a good-looking guy can be smart and interesting too," I said. "So Lucinda goes out with the second-best option: good-looking and—how shall I put it?—lacking what really counts."

"So you're saying I'm good-looking?" Mystery Guy said. Good grief. Had he missed everything I said?

"Well, you're no match for my hubby, but—"

"Touché," he said, smiling. "I'm Philip, by the way." He extended his hand.

"Sydney." We shook.

So I continued to fill him in on all of Lucinda's finer points, and eventually Philip took the bait and asked me for her e-mail address. "I think you'd have a really good time together," I said as I scribbled her information down.

"I'll take your word for it," Philip said. "It can't hurt to try, right?"

"Certainly not," I offered. "Well, I guess I should be going. Lucinda and I have some errands to run. But it was very nice to meet you."

"Likewise," Philip said. "Who knows, maybe Lucinda and I will hit it off, and we'll have you to thank!"

I sure hoped so, but in the meantime, I had to get back to Lucinda's. By the way, did I mention how good the bagel was? Why can't they have real New York bagels in Minnesota?

❃　❃　❃

The church office is chilly this morning . . .

Campbell had already been settled in his office for a couple of hours, working on his latest sermon series for the singles' group. The room, nestled in the church's basement, was cold and damp from the rain, but the green tea he'd been sipping helped to alleviate the chill.

Originally, he'd planned to talk about the always timely topic of personal finance management and stewardship, using his recent enrollment in Dave Ramsey's money management program as inspiration. When Campbell actually sat down to start fleshing it out, though, he just wasn't feeling it. For one reason or another, he couldn't get excited about writing about tithing or giving beyond your means, even as relevant as those topics always were. Instead, he was moved to talk about something even more personal, something he'd actually been wrestling with lately: maintaining a vibrant relationship with God unmotivated by legalism.

Campbell had been a Christian for most of his life. Some might say he didn't really have a choice in the matter: His father was a well-known pastor in the Minneapolis area, his mother a best-selling Christian author and speaker. So Campbell grew up hearing about God on a daily basis. And when he was five years old, his parents couldn't have been more proud when Campbell responded to an altar call during a Sunday night service at Elm Creek Baptist Church, the congregation his father still pastored today. That particular night, Campbell solidified his personal commitment to God, and from that day forward, he did his best to follow God's commands, no matter how uncool he seemed to those who didn't share his beliefs.

But lately, Campbell had been having what some people would call a crisis of faith. Granted, this was coming much later than it did for most people. Campbell never really went through a rebellious phase in high school, college, or even seminary for that matter, which was odd for a pastor's kid. Or at least the ones Campbell knew—the binge drinkers, the pot smokers, the let's-score-with-anyone-possible crowd. When it came to that proverbial checklist of rights and wrongs for Campbell, he was technically doing everything right. He never missed a Sunday at church, didn't drink excessively, lie, cheat on his taxes, or sleep around. But as anyone with even a rudimentary understanding of God's grace knows, growing in your faith isn't contingent upon following a strict set of rules. And that's where Campbell struggled. He knew plenty about God, enough to graduate with honors from seminary and to effectively lead the singles' group. But Campbell didn't always feel like he really knew God. That relationship, something his dad had preached about so many times, was what he longed for.

This wasn't something he'd ever shared with the group before. He'd always been the consummate professional and successfully maintained the illusion that he had everything together. Of course, no one expected him to be perfect. But his position of leadership and the high standards he held himself to didn't leave much room for no-holds-barred authenticity in his mind. Campbell thought if he dared to admit his struggles, he'd let the group down.

Somehow in the act of ministering, the vulnerability of the group members themselves began to minister to him. He remembered how Lila had openly shared about her inability to trust guys in relationships because of her troubled past. And then came Jackson's heartbreaking confession: During a particularly vulnerable moment, Jackson admitted that he hadn't been entirely truthful in the past about why he'd gotten divorced. He had been apt to blame his wife in the past, citing her tendency to bore easily as the reason for the split, but that night he'd talked about the way he blatantly disregarded his ex-wife's feelings during the course of their two-year marriage. And *that*, not the boredom, was what caused her to get so fed up that she filed for divorce.

Hearing story after story, week after week, slowly gave

Campbell the courage to admit that everything wasn't okay in his life. That he wanted to experience God in a way that he hadn't before. As Campbell began writing his uncensored thoughts down on paper, he felt better than he had in a good long while.

＊　＊　＊

Lucinda and I are running a few pre-lunch errands . . .

When I returned to Lucinda's place from the bagel shop, she was sitting at her kitchen table, nervously drumming her freshly painted nails on the table. "Where have you been, Syd?" she said. "I tried calling, I tried texting . . . I thought you'd been mugged or something."

"Calm down," I said, giggling at her impressive flair for the dramatic. "Unlike you, I can't get by on just a Diet Coke for breakfast. I had to have sustenance. So I grabbed a bagel and did a little matchmaking."

"Matchmaking?" Lucinda asked quizzically. "For who?"

"Don't you mean whom?" I said snidely. "And to think *you're* the editor here."

"Don't change the subject," Lucinda replied. "Whom were you matchmaking for?"

"You, actually," I said.

"Me?" Lucinda asked. "Well, he'd better be cute. And rich."

"I couldn't think of a tactful way to ask how his investment portfolio was doing, so I don't know if he's rich. But he *is* cute," I said before launching into a few choice bullet points. "He's probably six foot two. Hazel eyes. Dark hair. He was wearing a black pin-striped Hugo Boss suit with a light blue tie."

"Oooooh, Mr. Sharp Dresser," Lucinda said. "Sounds promising. So what's his real name?"

"Philip," I said.

"Philip. I like that," she replied. "He sounds refreshingly normal."

"Yeah, he was down-to-earth," I said. "But also good-looking, sweet, and funny."

"A formidable combo," Lucinda added before her ADD kicked in and she got off topic. "Should be interesting to see if he gets in touch. But now that you're back, we've really gotta jet. Lots of errands to run before lunch. A day off is rare for me."

"Don't you mean a personal day?" I asked. "I've always heard that most people actually work on Mondays."

"I work on plenty of Mondays," Lucinda said. "We just finished up a double issue, so I was dying for a day to myself."

"Fair enough," I said. "Do we have time for a bathroom break? I didn't have a chance when I was chattin' up Philip."

"Make it snappy," Lucinda said. Now she was the boss again.

After taking care of business and freshening up, probably less than five minutes but not nearly quick enough for Lucinda's naturally impatient nature, we hailed a cab. First stop? The Manolo Blahnik store on West Fifty-Fourth Street.

They'd just unveiled their fall line at a promo event, and I made myself useful by helping Lucinda pick out several new pairs (average price: a mere $482, although the majority of Lucinda's selections were much, much more—a serious jolt to the system of a frugal girl like me). Most people wouldn't be stocking up on their fall shoes and boots when it wasn't even summer yet, but Lucinda couldn't bear to be left behind on the latest fashions.

"It's a crime at *Vogue* to wear anything that's more than a year old," she informed me as she decided between the black, brown, and navy lace-up granny boots, this season's trendiest shoe.

"Well, it's a good thing I'm freelance," I replied. "The majority of my shoes are *at least* a year old. Guess they'd fire me on the spot."

"Quite possibly," Lucinda said with her trademark cackle. "Syd, you must get a pair. These fur-trimmed boots are just gorgeous."

"Um, they are, but I don't think they're in the budget right now," I said as I spotted the price tag. Only $1,200. That's more than our monthly mortgage!

"Oh, but Gavin would think they're divine, Syd," Lucinda cooed.

"I doubt Gavin would even know they were Manolos," I said. "He's not all that picky about my shoes, or his—Payless is just fine with him."

"Payless?" Lucinda exclaimed. Several salesgirls turned their heads in our direction. "That's ghastly. No one should ever be forced to wear those."

Embarrassed by the volume of Lucinda's voice, I turned my glance to the floor—all I knew to do in that uncomfortable moment. Then she spoke again, more softly this time. "Well, you're not leaving New York without those boots." She picked up the box. "And they're a steal too."

It's funny how my perspective and Lucinda's were so different on what's a steal and what's not. But I was now the proud owner of a pair of Manolos, a dream come true for a shoe lover like me.

Since there was no way we could lug around Lucinda's new collection of shoes (six pairs for her, one for me), Lucinda asked one of the salesgirls if she'd personally drop them by her apartment building. "No problem," the chipper blonde said as she stacked the boxes on top of each other and placed them in an oversized shopping bag. "They should be at your place within the hour."

I guess if you're an editor at Vogue, *customer service is taken to a whole new level,* I thought as I watched Lucinda in action. It was impressive yet unsettling at the same time.

"Perrrrfect," Lucinda cooed as she signed the credit card slip and impatiently handed it to the salesgirl.

The way she kept tapping her fingernails at the checkout counter indicated that she was clearly over the Manolo experience and ready for our next adventure. Even the salesgirl seemed to notice Lucinda's impatience and shot me a sympathetic look as if to say, *Better you than me.*

I smiled politely at the salesgirl, then turned to Lucinda. "Where to?"

"To eat, of course," Lucinda said. "I'm starving. Shoe shopping always makes me hungry. You know that, Sydney."

At that point, the salesgirl laughed out loud. And I giggled a little too. Sometimes Lucinda was just too much. Words like *high maintenance* were almost too kind. Full-on loony was a little more like it.

✱ ✱ ✱

Back in the comfort of her apartment . . .

Despite the gloominess of the day, Sam returned to her apartment in a rather happy state of mind after class. Everything had gone really well today. They'd had a study session for the final she'd be taking tomorrow for her Marriage and Family Therapy class, and for once she felt really good about a test.

Despite having good study habits, Samantha didn't consider herself the best test taker. Especially if it was a fill-in-the-bubble test. If she wasn't absolutely, positively sure about the answer, she would inevitably choose the wrong one, which was very frustrating. Essay tests, like the one tomorrow, were an entirely different matter. Samantha always felt more comfortable expressing her ideas in writing, something her professor had complimented her on recently in regard to her paper on the connection between birth order and long-term compatibility, one of her favorite research topics.

She and Eli had talked about and debated birth order at length, so this thought made her wonder how he was holding up. She knew it was none of her business since she'd been the one who'd ended things, but despite how horribly she'd acted, Samantha still cared about Eli and made sure to pray for him whenever he came to mind. Even so, she wasn't sure how to go about telling him how she felt without getting the brush-off (and understandably so) in return. Silence seemed like the best—and only—option.

Before Samantha's thoughts on Eli could get too carried way, however, her phone rang. It wasn't "Once in a Lifetime." Instead, Snow Patrol's "Chocolate" greeted her—the ringtone she'd chosen for Aidan. It was still all very strange but unexpectedly exciting at the same time. Samantha was surprised too by how elated she was to hear his voice again.

"Hello," she said brightly as she pushed her new bangs out of her face. Samantha was still wondering if this new fringe, as hip as it was right now, was really worth the hassle. No matter how many different ways she styled them, they always seemed to be in her eyes.

"Think I forgot about you?" Aidan said with a laugh.

Of course, Aidan had no idea how close to the truth that statement felt.

"Nah, I know your tricks by now. I figured you didn't want to seem overeager, right?" Sam said flirtatiously. "So what's new and exciting?"

"I'd tell you, but then I wouldn't have anything to talk about when I take you out for dinner tomorrow night," Aidan said. "You know, if you aren't busy."

Only one day's notice for a dinner invitation. Samantha knew what Sydney would say about that: *You can't be too available, Sam.*

Deciding not to cater to Aidan's every whim like she did the last time they dated, Samantha stayed strong. "You know, Aidan, I have plans for tomorrow night," she said coolly. "What if we shot for Thursday night instead?"

"How about seven o'clock?"

"'Perfect," Sam said. "Can't wait to catch up."

When they hung up a few minutes later, Samantha felt sublimely happy. She was getting the guy and holding on to her dignity in the process. What a concept.

❊   ❊   ❊

It's time for that working lunch with Lucinda . . .

After a longish cab ride in which we zigzagged through an endless stream of honking horns, Lucinda and I made our way to a chic bistro conveniently located on the ninth floor of Barneys New York. This was Lucinda's idea of heaven — five-star food and haute couture peacefully coexisting in the same regal quarters.

"I can't believe you haven't been here before, Syd," Lucinda said as we waited to be seated. "It's the place du jour for ladies who lunch."

"I'm sure it is, but it's not exactly convenient for someone who lives in Minnesota," I said with a laugh. "The commute would be brutal."

"I keep forgetting you live in the frozen tundra," Lucinda said. "You guys should seriously consider moving east—you'd adore it. And then, just think, we could come here all the time. You'd have no trouble getting a job, especially considering I know, well, *everyone* in the fashion biz."

Yeah, but I'm not sure I'd want to have lunch with you on a regular basis. Occasionally is hard enough to manage sometimes.

"Gavin likes it in Minneapolis, and so do I," I said. "So I don't think a move is in the works for a while. It's nice having the flexibility to travel here for work, though."

"Suit yourself," Lucinda said. "So . . . before I fill you in on that favor I need, you must decide what you're eating. I'd suggest the chicken noodle soup—it's the perfect food. It's tasty and virtually fat free."

"Tasty and fat free, that is pretty amazing," I said. "But I'm thinking the Penne alla Vodka is the way to go."

"Carbs, Syd, carbs. They are not your friends," Lucinda said. "How do you ever expect to fit into sample sizes if you're wolfing down pasta?"

"I can't say that being a size two or even a four has ever been one of my lifelong ambitions," I answered, much to Lucinda's dismay. "Believe it or not, I'm happy being an eight."

The waiter arrived before Lucinda could say any more. An

eight was practically plus-sized in her book. "I'll have the Penne alla Vodka," I said to the waiter. He was a dead ringer for Daniel Craig and probably a wannabe actor/model when he wasn't waiting tables.

"Excellent choice, madame," he said. "Not many women are brave enough to order something so decadent." Then, turning to Lucinda, "And for you, madame?"

"The chicken noodle soup, please," Lucinda said proudly. "I can't afford a meal of decadence."

I love how she isn't even subtle about taking a swipe. I guess it's better than talking behind my back, huh?

"Ah, that's too bad," he replied. "The sacrifices we make for beauty, eh?"

Clearly flattered by the interest of Mr. Bond, Lucinda cooed, "Oh, but the rewards are many." Her gaze lingered a few seconds too long, certainly on purpose. But he didn't seem to mind the attention as he flashed a crinkly smile in return.

After he walked away, I turned toward Lucinda. "You are shameless!" I said, reaching for a hearty slice of rosemary focaccia from the bread basket as Lucinda watched in horror.

"Well, I'd say he's quite the tasty treat. Definitely flirt-worthy." She laughed shortly.

"Yeah, if you want to repeat the whole Martin scenario," I offered. "Have you tried meeting any guys at church yet?"

"Well . . . that's exactly what I wanted to talk to you about," Lucinda began. "Remember that favor? Here's what I'm thinking . . ."

She began telling me about this up-and-coming Christian rock band called Stillness that she wanted me to interview for *Vogue*. Turns out she didn't meet them in church. Rather, it was during a Caribbean cruise a few months back—how random is that? Apparently they struck up a conversation after the band performed a late-night set and really hit it off.

"So what did they sound like?" I asked curiously. It would be helpful information if I was going to be writing about them.

Since Lucinda wasn't a music critic, though, she didn't have the easiest time describing their sound. "Um, I guess sort of rock, I think," she said. "But you can sing along to it. Does that help?"

"Sort of," I said. "That's definitely a start."

Despite Lucinda's lack of precision in describing Stillness's music, she was confident about one thing. "Syd, they've got faces that deserve to be seen by the masses."

I wasn't really sure what that meant, but I played along.

"So they're good-looking is what you're saying?" I said with a laugh. "Surprise, surprise."

Ignoring my wisecrack, Lucinda shifted into business mode. "They happen to be in town for promo stuff, so I'd like you to interview them tomorrow if you have time. They said afternoon was better than morning."

"Of course I have time, Lucinda," I said. "That's what I'm here for—to help you out. But I have to ask: A Christian band, no matter how talented it is, usually isn't *Vogue*'s first choice for coverage. What's the angle here?"

Just as she was about to answer, our food arrived, looking scrumptious. After she took a sip of her fat-free soup, Lucinda finally 'fessed up about her true intentions.

"Okay, okay, you know me too well," she began. "Of course they're talented, but off the record, I want you to set me up with Elton, their lead singer."

"Elton?" I asked with an impatient sigh. "As in the flamboyant piano-playing pop star? Seriously, Lucinda, you're trading editorial coverage for a *date*? That doesn't seem very professional."

"Sydney, I happen to recall your pining for one of your interview subjects for years," Lucinda shot back with a wicked grin. "You dated not once but twice before he married—"

I cut her off. "Yeah, I happen to remember that Liam's married, and I couldn't care less," I said. "All I'm saying is that maybe dating a guy in a band isn't the way to go."

"But he's a Christian, Syd, and I've never dated one of those before," Lucinda said. "You're always telling me that I need a relationship with a strong Christian man. And Elton more than qualifies. You'll see."

She had me there. Not wanting to prolong the inevitable (Lucinda wasn't one to give up easily, trust me), I relented. "Okay, breach of ethics or not, how do I go about getting in touch with Stillness?"

"That's my girl!" Lucinda said as she reached for her BlackBerry. "Here's their publicist's number."

CHAPTER 7

SHE ASKED FOR JUDE LAW, I GAVE HER JACK BLACK

What ever happened to responsible journalism?

— MAYOR KATE HENNINGS (CANDICE BERGEN) IN *SWEET HOME ALABAMA*,
2002

THE NEXT MORNING I woke up with a whopper of a headache. And despite my best efforts to get rid of the thing (extra-strength Tylenol, lying down, even applying minty aromatherapy lotion to my temples), the pain in my head wouldn't go away. Maybe it's because I was running around Manhattan with my pain-in-the-butt client all day yesterday, and I'd stayed up way too late strategizing after Lucinda basically asked me to fix her up with the lead singer of the band I was supposed to be interviewing today. How in the world was I going to naturally work in, "So, Elton, remember Lucinda? I think you two should go out some-time" into the conversation? I mean, c'mon, I love matchmaking, but this seemed a little crazy even to me. And that's saying a lot.

Aside from the aforementioned flirting with Liam in a Q&A that happened years and years ago now (for the record, the friendly banter went both ways, and Liam was the one who asked me out, not the other way around), I've always been the epitome of professionalism during my interviews. And I will say this: That's not always easy. Especially if you happen to be talking to the cast of *Lost* or your first-ever crush, Simon Le Bon from Duran Duran. But somehow I've always been able to hold it together and stick with the five *W*s of journalism—who, what, when, where, and why—instead of coming across like the superfan I am.

But as much as I wanted to bail on Operation Elton, I was sure I'd figure something out because, unfortunately, Lucinda was someone who demanded results. And *Vogue* was my biggest client. If I came back without passing along her phone number, e-mail address, or something that would ensure the two of them were going on at least one date sometime in the near future, she was going to wonder what went wrong on my end. Because, of course, it'll be my fault if Elton doesn't fall madly in love with her.

Arrrrgh! Why couldn't I have a normal editor like everyone else? One who didn't want me prying into her private business. One who simply edited a little too heavily or had an annoying quirk like an overly nasal voice or the bad habit of giving me unreasonable deadlines. Instead, I've got a boss who wants me to set her up on dates with much younger men named Elton.

❋ ❋ ❋

Strumming away in Minneapolis . . .

One thousand miles from the frenetic pace of New York City, Gavin was holed up in his studio, working on a new song and missing his wife. Sure, it had only been a couple of days, but it just wasn't the same without Sydney around. Gavin knew she was probably having fun in the Big Apple with Lucinda, as neurotic as she was, but he really couldn't wait for Sydney to come home tomorrow. For some reason, whenever they were apart, he was more introspective than usual (and probably not in a good way).

As he repeatedly tried to come up with lyrics to match the pretty but pensive melody he'd been strumming nearly nonstop for the past few days, Gavin fought what had been a recurring problem lately: writer's block.

Whenever Gavin was working with Jaguar or any number of artists he'd helped on a freelance songwriting basis, he never struggled to find the catchy turn of phrase to express exactly what they hoped to convey. In fact, it was the reason he was hired again and again. Whether they needed a sullen song about the hard knocks of love or an upbeat ditty about its pure elation, he was the go-to guy.

Like anyone who loved songwriting as much as Gavin, however, he wasn't satisfied with simply penning songs for other people, no matter how good they ended up being; he wanted to make his personal contribution to the music scene. He looked up to singer-songwriters like Bob Dylan and Paul Westerberg, artists who weren't content with anything but gritty songs straight from the heart.

But aside from the recent love song he wrote for Sydney, which he still didn't consider finished, Gavin found it difficult to write new material that really mattered to him. Frankly, now that his life was in such a happy place, especially with his new marriage, it wasn't easy to craft something with any emotional depth at all. It all felt too silly, too contrived. And he didn't like it one bit.

Strangely enough, so many times when Gavin found himself at a loss for words for a new song these days, his old roommate

John Elias would pop into his head.

Before he met Sydney, Gavin shared a three-bedroom apartment with John, who'd given up his career as a criminal lawyer two years ago to pursue a degree in secondary education. At first, Gavin couldn't believe that John would walk away from such a lucrative career. It wasn't like John hated what he did. He didn't dread going to work every day. The pay was generous—really generous. It allowed him to have a comfortable life. But the more clients he worked with for months on end, the more John believed there was something more for him to do with his life. He was in his midthirties, was single, and knew without a shadow of a doubt that he didn't want to be a lawyer for the rest of his life.

So after praying about it for a few months and consulting with his pastor and others close to him whom he trusted implicitly, John quit the law firm and embarked on a new adventure. And even though Gavin vowed he'd never go back to school for an advanced degree, he couldn't shake the thought that maybe his writer's block was happening for a reason. Not like God was punishing him or anything like that—he hated it when people suggested silly stuff like that in the midst of a trying time. Rather, Gavin saw it as an opportunity to examine what his next steps might be, career-wise—and if those would even include anything music-related at all.

* * *

An unexpected meeting at Panera . . .

Jane was definitely feeling under the weather when she woke up that morning, but the news never called in sick, so it wasn't an option for her either. But as soon as she wrapped up her morning show duties around eleven, her boss actually sent her home—*quelle surprise*!

Even though her throat was sore and she was sure she had a mild fever, Jane found the rumblings of her hungry stomach difficult to ignore. Knowing she didn't have anything but a carton of soy milk, salad dressing, and maybe some orange juice in her fridge, Jane decided to pick up lunch—soup from Panera. It was only a few blocks from her place; surely she could keep from falling asleep at the wheel for that long.

Pulling into the parking lot, Jane noticed what a gorgeous day it was, and she was disappointed she couldn't enjoy it more. The sun was shining brightly, the flowers were in full bloom, and here she was, sicker than a dog. Retrieving a tissue from her purse and heading inside, she didn't even notice who was standing in line near the register until he said her name three times.

"Jane, is that you?" asked a handsome guy with a huge grin on his face.

In her achy, sleepy state, it took Jane a second to figure out who it was. Once she did, her heart started to race. It was Campbell.

"Hi," Jane began. "I'm a bit slow today—not feeling the best at the moment."

"I'm sorry to hear that," Campbell said. "Anything I can do to make you feel better?"

Jane thought of several things. *Yeah, you could ask me on a date. Ask me to be your wife. Ask me to run away with you somewhere romantic like Tuscany. . . . Okay, I'm getting carried away.*

"Nothing immediately springs to mind, but thanks for your concern," Jane said with as much energy as she could muster. "Wanna join me for a bowl of soup?"

"I'm more of a panini guy myself, but I'd still like your company," Campbell said. "What kind of soup do you want? My treat."

"That's really sweet of you, Campbell. Broccoli cheese would be perfect," Jane said, wondering if this technically qualified as a date. "Thank you."

"You're welcome," Campbell said. "Now go find us a place to sit so you can rest."

Go find us *a place to sit.* Jane really liked the sound of that.

✻ ✻ ✻

Interview in process . . .

Since Stillness was relatively new to the music scene and *Vogue* was the magazine the band was going to be featured in, it didn't take long at all to set up an interview. Only one phone call, a true rarity in this biz.

Picking a place to meet, however, wasn't nearly as easy. After going back and forth with the band's manager via e-mail for the better part of an hour, we eventually settled on the Dean & DeLuca on Broadway, a much-buzzed-about coffee emporium that also sells high-end treats like foie gras, specialty cheeses (Brie, anyone?), and five-dollar chocolate-covered strawberries. And while I'm positive I'll never have the urge to try foie gras (the fattened livers of geese and ducks that have been force-fed a mixture of corn, lard, and salt water), I just had to see what was so spectacular about these particular chocolate-covered strawberries to warrant such a markup.

Once I arrived and settled in, I definitely had bigger matters than those strawberries to ponder. I was still trying to figure out how I was going to score Lucinda that date with Elton. Before I could give the issue much more thought, I spotted two guys who had to be Elton and one of his bandmates. Unlike the majority of the bands I interview on a regular basis, these guys were actually five minutes early and didn't have their publicist in tow. Amazing.

Elton looked exactly like Lucinda had described him. Tall and good-looking in that traditional, model-like way, he carried himself with confidence as he scanned the room. Elton could probably pass for an NFL celebrity quarterback of the Tom Brady/Tony Romo ilk—the sort of guy who'd throw a record number of touchdowns every Sunday and still have time to cavort around with enough supermodels to grace the pages of *Us Weekly* on a regular basis.

His cohort, though not as strikingly attractive as Elton, was cute in more of an all-American, approachable way. His lanky, decidedly unmuscular frame led me to believe he wasn't ever much of an athlete but found his niche in playing music. I guessed he's the guy in the group who probably listens to music all the time and keeps up with all the trends and techie gadgets so his bandmates don't have to. That, of course, doesn't leave much time for relationships, so my guess was that he's single. But he's definitely looking for something a little more substantial than a quick fling. Basically, he's the kind of man I'd much prefer to set Lucinda up with.

It's funny how much you can assume just from looking at someone. I began wondering how many of these deductions were actually fact and how many were fiction. I waved and they walked over in my direction.

"Sydney?" Elton asked politely.

"Yep, I'm Sydney. You must be Elton."

"You're right on the money," Elton said. "This is Nick, my bass player."

"*Your* bass player, huh?" Nick jokingly said in response. "Front men. They're all the same, aren't they, Sydney? Think the world revolves around them."

"Isn't that the truth?" I shot back with a laugh. "I used to date one. But I'm sure Elton's not that self-absorbed."

"Well, I don't know about *that*," Elton said. "Guess you'll just have to judge for yourself."

"Sounds like a plan," I said. "Shall we get started?"

Quickly segueing back into professional mode, I asked the band if they wanted anything to munch on before we began. As it turned out, they knew the magazine-pays-for-all-the-goodies drill all too well, as they ordered what amounted to a veritable feast (including six of those aforementioned strawberries).

With coffee and delectable treats in tow, we eventually ventured back to a free table and began our official interview. The setup was comfortable, even with the noisy ambience, and like the majority of the Q&As I've conducted over the years, I found a comfortable, chatty rapport with the band.

Although I've managed to have good luck most of the time, I've definitely learned a few tricks of the trade while interviewing celebrities (or in this case, celebrities in training) over the years. As long as you're talking about a subject that's interesting to them or one that's been rigorously prepared for in media training sessions, everything goes swimmingly. But if you veer too far off the beaten path into uncharted territory, things go sour—and fast. Since this was a get-to-know-you piece for *Vogue*, however, there wasn't much potential for drama. Well, aside from getting a date for Lucinda. Which, by the way, wasn't going particularly well at all. I'd yet to find even one open window for broaching the subject.

As the interview began to wind down after an hour and a half or so, I asked them what was up next in terms of touring. My salvation finally arrived just in the nick of time.

"Don't get me wrong, I've always loved touring, and I don't anticipate that changing anytime soon," Elton began. "But since I started dating my girlfriend a couple of months ago, I've been reminded yet again that there's ultimately so much more to life than our music. Spending time with her has provided me with a more balanced perspective on what's important and what's not. So we've decided on several smaller two-week stretches instead of one big tour for our promotion."

He has a girlfriend. Hallelujah. Now I wouldn't have to bother slipping in that part about going out with Lucinda.

"Funny how the right girl can do that, huh?" I replied. "Sounds like a good decision." Then turning to Nick, I asked, "So how about you, Nick? Someone special to help keep you focused?"

"I haven't had a date in ages," Nick confessed. "I probably spend too much time online and listening to music to meet the right girl. But, hey, if you know anyone cute, I'm always open to suggestions."

Well, look at that. Not only was I right about Nick being Mr. Techie, but here was my open window. Surely Lucinda wouldn't mind going out with Nick. He wasn't Elton, but he certainly seemed like a worthy eligible bachelor.

"In that case, I think you should meet my editor," I said, testing the waters. "She definitely wouldn't disappoint."

"Yeah, I remember meeting her on the cruise," Elton said

to Nick. "She was cute, sophisticated, and funny in that self-deprecating way."

"There's an offer I can't refuse: Cute. Sophisticated. Funny," Nick said. "So, speaking hypothetically, uh, how would I get in touch with her, Sydney?"

"I'd start with e-mail," I said. "Lucinda always has her BlackBerry with her. That way, you could get to know each other a little first *before* going out."

"I like that," Nick said. "Find out all the basics so you can talk about more important things later."

"Exactly," I said.

"I'd say I rather liked this interview," Nick said to Elton. "A feature in *Vogue* and a setup all in one afternoon."

"Yeah, you can't beat that," Elton said. "Thanks so much for everything, Sydney."

"No problem," I said. "It was a pleasure hanging out. For the record, I love setting people up. It's one of my favorite things to do."

"Really?" Nick asked. "You sound like my cousin Lucy. You know the advice column 'Lucy for the Lovelorn'?"

"You mean the nationally syndicated newspaper column?" I asked enthusiastically.

"Yeah, that's the one," Nick said. "I guess you've seen it."

"Seen it? I love it! She gives the best advice," I said. "So Lucy likes setting people up too?"

"It's practically her second job," Nick said. "She's probably set me up four or five times."

"That's funny—I always joke that it's my second job too," I said. "Any of these setups actually a success?"

"Most of them were duds," Nick said. He made a face. "But

I dated Jessica for almost two years. Things went really well until I realized she was much farther down the path to marital bliss than I was. There really hasn't been anyone since."

"I'm sorry to hear that," I offered. "It's never easy when two people have different expectations."

"No kidding," Nick said as he played with the ends of his chin-length hair. "But who knows? Maybe Lucinda and I will hit it off."

"Crazier things have happened, " I said with a laugh. "And you'll have me to thank."

"If something great happens, you'll be the first one I thank."

After talking for a few more minutes, the guys and I went our separate ways. All in all, the day had been a success. Or at least I hoped that's what Lucinda would think when I filled her in on the slight change of plans.

* * *

Jane can't stop smiling . . .

Lunch with Campbell ended up being a wonderfully unexpected surprise for Jane. Normally when she wasn't feeling well, she wanted nothing more than to be at home snoozing away with her fluffy down comforter pulled up to her neck.

But Campbell's company was a great substitute for a cozy blanket as they shared lunch and meaningful conversation. Moving beyond surface chatter, they talked about their jobs, and Campbell filled her in about what he planned to talk about in small group tonight.

"I think that's something we can all relate to," Jane said. "It's easy to shy away from being vulnerable when you're the leader. But I think in the long run that's what will make you a better one. I've definitely experienced similar spiritual struggles, so I'm sure there are others in the group who have too."

"That's good to hear," Campbell said. "I didn't want to cross over into the dreaded oversharing category."

"No, I'm pretty sure that wouldn't be classified as oversharing," Jane said, smiling. "Now, if you showed everyone your feet, like one of my dates did recently, that would be crossing the line."

"You're kidding. Some guy showed you his feet on a date?" Campbell asked.

"Yeah, and we were eating guacamole at the time," Jane said. "Needless to say, I lost my appetite and any interest I could've had in him."

"Understandable," Campbell offered. "So how did you meet this guy? The whole situation has blind date written all over it."

"How did you guess?" Jane said. "Sydney introduced us. Weston is in Gavin's touring band, and I guess he'd always acted perfectly normal. Until he went out with me, of course. I have that effect on men sometimes."

"I'm sure it's not you," Campbell said, his cheeks turning slightly red. "You're lovely."

"You're making me blush," Jane said, her voice trembling just a little. "Thank you."

While flushed cheeks and unexpected compliments could've made the next few minutes awkward, Campbell and Jane just kept right on talking. Then around two o'clock, when Jane started feeling even worse, she decided she'd better take off.

"It's been so fun hanging out, Campbell, but if I don't get to bed soon, I probably won't be able to come to group tonight," Jane said.

"We can't have that," Campbell said. "Let me walk you to your car."

"You don't have to do that. I'll be fine," Jane said confidently as she gathered her purse and a small to-go container with the soup she hadn't finished.

"I know you'll be fine, but I want to," Campbell replied in a tone that hinted at feelings that weren't strictly platonic. Then, as if to underscore (or at least confirm) her suspicions, Campbell gave Jane a quick but friendly hug before she got into her car and headed home. "Hope to see you later," he said. "But if not, we'll pray for you."

When Campbell gave her the hug, Jane caught a whiff of his cologne close to his neck. It was yummy (and not overpowering, an important distinction). And even though she was now in her car, she could still smell a trace of it on her own shirtsleeve, a pleasant reminder of an unexpected outing with the guy she had a crush on—a crush that was growing exponentially with each encounter.

* * *

Bringing Lucinda up to speed on the day's events . . .

When I got back to Lucinda's gorgeous Manhattan flat overlooking Central Park, I happily had the place to myself. While I hadn't done anything particularly strenuous today, short of walking a few blocks to hail a cab, I was exhausted from all the pre-interview worrying. My head had stopped aching hours ago, but I felt like I could use a good long nap.

I was guessing a catnap would have to do, though. Lucinda had texted me a couple of times during the interview to let me know when we'd be heading out to dinner. First it was seven thirty at Nobu, but when reservations proved too difficult to secure at the popular sushi joint, even for an editor at *Vogue*, Lucinda decided Mexican was the way to go.

Since it was only five thirty, I assumed I'd have about an hour to chill before Lucinda would be ready to head out since she usually got off work around six o'clock. I'd just thrown off a mountain of pillows and settled into her plush, oversized sofa with a Diet Coke and sole possession of the remote control to her high-def plasma screen TV when Lucinda arrived home like the tornado ripping through Kansas in *The Wizard of Oz*. Apparently it had been a bad day at work.

"What's up?" I offered as she threw a light jacket and her purse on her gorgeous cherry dining room table.

"I'm in desperate need of a margarita," Lucinda said. "It's been a stressful day. My boss, Ted—the one we call the flesh-eating copyeditor because he thinks he knows more than the copyediting team—didn't like our summer getaway advertorial with Rachel McAdams on the cover, so I have to start over from scratch."

"From scratch? What's your deadline?" I asked sympathetically, knowing how crazy magazine production schedules can be.

"We have three days, Sydney! *Three days!*" Lucinda roared. "And they're wanting me to get a new copywriter because Ted thinks the one we hired can't write to save her life."

"Wow, that is tragic. Bring on the margarita," I offered. "Anything I can do to help?"

"Yeah — wanna write the darn thing?" Lucinda said. "You'd be a lifesaver if you did."

"Well, I'm flying home tomorrow, of course. But after I get back, I could do a quick turnaround for you," I said.

"Perfect," Lucinda said. "I'll put you in touch with Rachel's people for a phoner and give you the rest of the details later."

"Sounds good," I said.

I'm fairly sure Lucinda didn't hear that last sentence, though, as she made a beeline to her room to primp for dinner.

I didn't really worry about gussying up myself. My interview outfit had already been approved by Lucinda this morning (just one of the many interesting quirks I had to endure when I stayed with her), so I thought I'd save the trouble of hearing her opinion a second time and stick with the same threads, which included the fab fur-lined new Manolo boots. Seriously, I was in love.

I've always fancied myself a bit of a fashionista. I love shoes, scarves, skirts, purses, you name it. But since I'm a fashionista on a budget, Lucinda doesn't always approve of my wardrobe choices. While I'm always thrilled to find a bargain at Banana Republic, Bloomingdale's, or (gasp!) TJ Maxx, couture is the only option for Lucinda, so occasionally she'll tell me that my outfit "looks a little cheap." That comment would definitely offend some people, but I'm more than used to it, and when she does get under my skin, I politely remind her that most of her couture these days comes courtesy of the wardrobe closet at *Vogue*. Because Lucinda covers designer brands like Chanel, Gucci, and Dolce & Gabbana on a regular basis, she gets access to all the exclusive promo goodies they send. As a freelancer, these perks are few and far between for me, so I'd have to pay full price, which is ridiculous. As gorgeous as a hand-banded Chanel gown is, I hardly think it's worth nine thousand dollars. Call me crazy, but I can think of hundreds of ways that money could be better utilized.

When I was midway through an episode of "Project Runway" that Lucinda had TiVo'ed, she was finally ready to head out. "You look nice, Sydney," she said as she scanned my outfit. "Love the lip gloss. MAC, I presume?"

"Yep, the shade's called Enchantress, if you're interested," I said.

"I'll have to try that," she said as she ran a brush through her hair and spritzed herself with perfume. Then she picked up her phone and called a cab.

"You're looking good, considering you're just hangin' with me tonight," I said to Lucinda after she hung up the phone.

"Well, you never know who you're going to see at this restaurant," Lucinda said, her eyes sparkling. "Jessica Simpson always brings whoever she's dating there. And once I saw John Cusack sitting there all by himself, noshing on chips and salsa."

"Ooooh, did you walk up and talk to him? Tell him you'd never give him a pen if he gave you his heart?" I said jokingly.

"What are you talking about?" Lucinda asked grumpily.

"It's from *Say Anything...*, one of John Cusack's biggest movies," I said. "Don't tell me you've never seen it."

"You know I don't have the time or patience for movies," Lucinda remarked. "I haven't seen a movie in a couple of years."

"That's too bad," I said as we walked toward Lucinda's front door. "You gotta take some time for you every once in a while. It can't be all work, work, work."

"I know," she said. "That's one of the reasons I wanted you to set me up with Elton. Get my mind off the office. How did that go, by the way? Does he have all my pertinent information?"

Ummm. Maybe Lucinda needs to have that margarita—a good strong margarita—before I tell her.

I paused a minute, collecting my thoughts, and then said, "I'll fill you in at the restaurant. Sound good?" The cab was waiting out front anyway.

"Sure," Lucinda said. "So I wanted to surprise you, since it's your last night here and all. I got fourth row comps today for the nine o'clock showing of *Legally Blonde on Broadway*. Sound like fun?"

"Totally! Thank you so much!" I said. "I haven't been to a play since I did that last piece for *Get Away*."

"Thought you'd like it," Lucinda said. "I haven't been to a play since I've lived in Manhattan, can you believe that?"

"That's truly a shame," I said. "I think I'd be tempted to go all the time if I lived here."

"Yet another reason you and Gavin need to move," Lucinda said. "Seriously, you two should consider it."

Lucinda and I had talked about that many times before, and my answer never changed. Fortunately, we'd arrived at our destination, so I was off the hook (as far as that conversation went, anyway).

The restaurant was definitely not slacking in the cool ambience department. Chic and dimly lit, the dark wood and red accents gave it a classy, upscale feel, which isn't the vibe one normally associates with a place known for its Tex-Mex. And the place was hopping. In fact, it was so noisy that it was hard to carry on a conversation—which could prove to be a good thing, depending on how Lucinda reacted to my news that

Elton was already taken.

After we were seated and our drink orders were taken, Lucinda simply couldn't wait another minute. "You've been stalling. What's the deal with Elton?"

"He seemed really nice and gave some great quotes for the article, but he's already got a girlfriend," I said nervously.

"So what?" Lucinda said emphatically. "If they aren't married, he's still fair game. You still could've given him my number."

"You're right, they aren't married—but he did seem really crazy about her," I replied. "He's even shortening the band's tour run so he can spend more time with her."

"Awww, isn't that sweet?" Lucinda said sarcastically. "Guess I'm just a little disappointed. With you being the crackerjack at setting people up, I thought for sure you'd knock this one way out of the park."

"Well, there's only so much one can do when a girlfriend's in the mix," I said. "But I did the next best thing."

"What's that?" Lucinda asked. "Does he have a twin brother?"

"Nope, but the band's bassist, Nick, is cute and *single*, so I gave him your e-mail address," I said. "He seemed like your ty—"

"I met Nick on the cruise, and I'm sure he's nice." Lucinda looked a little miffed. "But I asked for Jude Law, and you basically gave me Jack Black. Real life isn't like *The Holiday*, where a girl like Kate Winslet falls in love with a goofy guy like Jack Black. It just isn't."

When Lucinda was finished with her little tirade, she took out her BlackBerry and absently started typing. Then, without even making eye contact, she said, "Do you understand why I'm frustrated here?"

Thanks to Lucinda's snarky comment, I felt like I was about six years old. "It definitely wasn't my intention to set you up with Jack Black," I began. "I actually thought Nick was cute and charming. I thought he'd be a nice change from your norm—which never seems to work out. But apparently I was way off."

Before Lucinda had a chance to respond, our waiter mixed a bowl of spicy guacamole right at the table. Thick and chunky just the way I like it, I couldn't resist trying some immediately. Even Lucinda, who normally avoids like the plague anything that resembles a chip, scooped up a generous portion. Those smashed-up avocados must have made her happier somehow because her tone immediately softened.

"My comment was probably a little out of line. I'm sorry about that, Syd," she said. "Nothing seems to be going right lately, and the thought of going out with Elton really excited me. Now that's not happening either. It's like I have the reverse Midas touch. Everything I touch turns to . . . I don't know. Brass."

"I've definitely been there," I offered sympathetically. "And that's why it couldn't hurt to broaden your relational horizons."

"I know, I know," she said. "I hate it when you're right. You're just too practical for me sometimes."

"I know," I said. "I just want you to be happy, that's all."

"I appreciate that," Lucinda said. "By the way, did I tell you that I've been e-mailing Philip? I think we're going to go out for coffee later this week."

"That sounds like a positive development," I said with a grin. "Are you liking the conversation so far?"

"Well, he doesn't sound like an axe murderer," Lucinda said. "But he did suggest coffee first, which makes me think he doesn't want to shell out the big bucks until he meets me for the first time."

I laughed; Lucinda was something else.

"There's nothing wrong with a coffee date," I said. "Gavin and I met at a coffee shop, and it worked out okay for us. Maybe there's something magical in lattes that naturally brings people closer together."

"Like what?" Lucinda said in her cynical tone. "Milk? Espresso shots? Maybe it's the caramel drizzle."

"A date is a date, Lucinda. And just think, if I hadn't gone out for a carb fix, you wouldn't have met Philip at all," I said. "See, carbs aren't always the enemy."

"Point taken. But I'll have to get back to you on that after Philip and I go out," Lucinda said. "Who knows? I may just hate carbs more than ever."

CHAPTER 8

THE RISKY ROAD TO FORGIVENESS

What's the word that's burning in your heart?

—SAM (NATALIE PORTMAN) IN *GARDEN STATE*, 2004

WHILE I'M DEFINITELY A card-carrying member of the I-Love-NYC fan club, I can't even begin to tell you how happy I was to be heading back home to Minneapolis.

I missed Gavin. I missed the sanity of everyday life without Lucinda and all her drama. I missed being in a city of manageable size where I actually recognize some familiar faces from time to time. Oh, and have I mentioned that I missed Gavin? Honestly, I don't know how I ever lived without him.

All in all, my trip to New York was a success, though. I accomplished exactly what I went to do: I caught up with Lucinda, did some work, and got in a little shopping too. After the rocky start to our evening last night, Lucinda and I actually left on good terms. Even though I wasn't able to set her up with "the man of her dreams," I did give her e-mail address to two eligible bachelors, not too shabby for just a few days' work. And for the record, I'm fairly confident that Elton wasn't actually the man of Lucinda's dreams anyway. My guess is that even if he'd been single, she would've moved on to someone else in no time flat. Unfortunately, Lucinda's attention span is short with just about everything—especially men. And unless they were cheating on her or treating her poorly (oh, the irony!), she'd discard them as quickly as last season's shoes.

I was curious to see how things would go with her and Philip, though. At first I wasn't sure about his potential. But when he mentioned Bible study, I started to think he had the right stuff for a real relationship. It would be interesting to see what, if anything, became of that curious meeting in the bagel shop.

In the meantime, though, I couldn't wait for my plane to board. I'd close my eyes, nod off to dreamland, and before long, I'd be home at last.

＊　＊　＊

Eli enjoys a midmorning celebratory breakfast at Perkins . . .

Eli had just wrapped up the last final exam of his college career and decided to celebrate by getting blueberry pancakes at a nearby Perkins. He'd just pulled an all-nighter and hadn't eaten anything but peanut M&Ms since lunch, so, needless to say, he was starving.

He'd asked a couple of friends to join him, but neither was particularly interested in food at the moment—after cramming for exams, sleep was the only thing that was important to them. Despite their repeated encouragement that Eli grab some z's of his own, his friends' disinterest didn't sway him. So he ventured to Perkins alone.

Alone. That was a word that Eli was far too familiar with lately. After he and Sam had broken up, Eli felt reclusive, even though it had only been four days. The last thing he wanted was to be the downer in his group of friends, so he avoided most social interaction: parties, dinner invitations, Bible study, you name it. Unfortunately for him, his friends began picking up on this very new habit of his and forced him to get out of his apartment anyway. Of course, Eli knew it was good for him to get out, but the real world wasn't always easy to face when everything seemed to remind him of his ex.

He'd drive pass the AMC Theater in the Rosedale Mall and remember all the movies they'd seen together. Across the street was the Chili's where they'd shared countless conversations over bottomless chips and salsa and Diet Coke. Just down the road was the Dunn Bros coffee shop where he and Sam played Scrabble and drank lattes together on the weekends. Just seeing these places conjured up memories he was now eager to forget.

But as Eli sipped his decaf (so he could go to sleep after he got back home) and took bite after bite of the delicious pancakes, he couldn't help but think of the sermon he'd heard last Sunday morning about harboring unforgiveness. When Eli'd first picked up on what his pastor was speaking about, he promptly began planning an early exit. But since he happened to be sitting right in the middle of a crowded row of families, he rethought his strategy and wondered if God might be trying to say something to him.

The sermon's scriptural text centered around the account of Jesus' crucifixion found in Matthew. While the details of the passage were familiar to him, the pastor's practical insight on forgiveness that resulted wasn't something to which Eli had given much thought.

The pastor elaborated on how Jesus didn't think twice about forgiving everyone from Judas (who'd betrayed him for thirty pieces of silver) to the angry crowd (who chose to release a murderer named Barabbas instead of the innocent Son of God) to his disciple Peter (who denied him not once but three times, even though Peter had spent several years as Jesus' follower). "Really, if anyone deserved to hold a grudge against these people, it was Jesus," the pastor had said. "And if Jesus had the capacity to forgive them, surely there's someone in your life you could make the same gesture for, right?"

Eli knew that person in his life with Samantha. And Aidan too, if he was honest with himself. But of the two, it was Samantha Eli had the hardest time forgiving. The wound was still so fresh, and, frankly, he expected Aidan to act like a jerk. But it was out of character for Sam to leave with so little in the way of explanation, especially when their relationship had been going so well. But Eli hadn't given her much time to explain. And no matter how many times his friends told him it wasn't his fault, Eli couldn't help but think it was somehow. If he'd been more exciting, more dangerous, more . . . *something*, surely Samantha wouldn't have gone back to Aidan.

Before his thoughts could travel down that destructive road yet again, Eli put down his fork and prayed for strength. And then he added an unexpected postscript to his prayer. *God, I want you to know that I not only forgive Sam and Aidan, but if they would be truly happy together, I want that for them too.*

Eli didn't feel an instant rush of happiness after what he'd just prayed, but ultimately he knew he'd done the right thing. And maybe, just maybe, that would free him up to move on and evaluate what the next phase of his life was going to look like—even if it didn't involve Samantha.

＊　＊　＊

Exams are a wrap for Sam too . . .

Across campus, Sam was now officially finished with her finals too. She was excited that she wouldn't have to take another test at Bethel University, but still she felt unsettled somehow. She couldn't believe that this was really the end of her undergraduate days. Her season at Bethel University was coming to a close, and that felt strange and surreal. The comfortable bubble she'd lived in for four years was about to burst, thrusting her smack-dab into the real world. And unlike college — with student loan payments on hold and a slew of friends just a short walk down the hallway — the real world was full of uncertainties.

Would she have enough money to make that pesky loan payment every month? Where would she live, and what, exactly, would she do for a living? Would she stay in touch with the same circle of friends she had at Bethel? Or would she be forced to start from scratch and make new ones? There were so many questions.

So Samantha thought she'd busy herself with errands in the meantime. After all, what's better than avoidance when your life is filled with so many unanswered questions? First up was a trip to her campus post office box. With all the stress leading up to finals week, she hadn't checked its contents in a few days.

As Samantha turned the key and pulled out a huge batch of envelopes, she sighed. Her Visa bill was sitting right on top. Samantha dreaded the arrival of her Visa bill the way most people dreaded a checkup at the dentist. Like the times you know you haven't flossed nearly enough, yet still hope the dental hygienist will go easy on the scraping, Sam knew her retail therapy had gone way out of control last month. Yet that didn't stop her from daydreaming about a few of her splurges somehow going unnoticed . . .

Maybe the salesgirl at Sephora made a mistake and forgot to charge my card. You know, like . . . human error. Or maybe Visa was undergoing a new software update and my bill was accidentally wiped clean. Imagine that! Maybe someone set the Visa building on fire in a fit of rage, and my bill was among those lost because they weren't smart enough to back up. Or—

No such luck. Her bill was right around the five-hundred-dollar mark. Just like she'd estimated.

With all that had been going on lately, Samantha was stressed. And like so many girls, Samantha believed that new lip gloss, sandals, and cute outfits for dates would be the cure-all for times like these. In hindsight? Not so much. But it seemed like a good idea at the time.

Moving the dreaded Visa bill to the bottom of the pile, Samantha riffled through the rest of the mail. Credit card offer. *Um, no thanks.* An invitation to a friend's upcoming bridal shower. *That'll be fun; bring on the party games and sparkling punch.* A letter from the University of Minnesota's psychology department. *Ooooh, what do they have to say?*

> *Dear Ms. Alexander,*
> *Congratulations! We are pleased to inform you*
> *that after reviewing your application, you've been*
> *accepted into the master's program for psychology*
> *at the University of Minnesota's College of*
> *Education & Human Development for the fall*
> *semester. Because of your continued commitment*
> *to academic excellence and research in the field of*

*marriage and family therapy, we are pleased to
offer you a generous scholarship that's renewable
each semester as long as you remain in good
academic standing. All the pertinent financial
details are included on the next page.*

*If you have any questions or concerns, feel free
to contact us at your convenience.*

Sincerely,

*Emma Rains, admissions counselor, University
of Minnesota*

Happy to get the good news but not ecstatic, Samantha leafed
through the rest of the mail: a form to fill out for the upcoming
commencement ceremony, the latest issue of *In Style*, a letter
from Denver Missions Institute. *Wait a minute. I never applied at
Denver Missions Institute. I wonder what they want.*

Dear Ms. Alexander,

*One of your professors, Dr. Kate Wallace,
mentioned that you might be a great fit for our
brand-new partnership program with schools in
Chennai, India. Our multifaceted program here
at Denver Missions Institute, which includes
extensive cultural and language training, would
equip you to teach English as a Second Language
(ESL) along with providing biblical studies
workshops and practical job skills in several
new Christian facilities that have opened up in
Chennai recently.*

Financial assistance and scholarships are

available for top candidates like yourself, so we'd encourage you to apply as soon as possible for a few remaining slots for the fall.

If you have any questions about this once-in-a-lifetime opportunity to make a difference in the lives of those in Chennai, feel free to contact us.
Sincerely,
Jacob Myers, admissions counselor, Denver Missions Institute

After reading the letter from Denver Missions Institute, Samantha seriously began to get excited about the opportunity she was being offered. It was so like Dr. Wallace to do something like that. For one reason or another, whenever Samantha told her about possibly pursuing a career as a marriage and family counselor, Dr. Wallace had never been a big fan. Dr. Wallace said it was definitely a worthy pursuit, but she believed that anyone with a heart for missions like Samantha had, especially in a place like India, should pursue that—even if only for a few years.

As a former missionary herself, Dr. Wallace always said her experiences as a teacher in Taiwan continued to shape her life. And when Samantha really thought about it, that sounded like something she wanted—a life-altering experience, even if the path wasn't predictable like it would be if she went to the U of M. *Decisions, decisions.* Samantha knew she had a lot of praying to do. And even if she did go for the India option, Aidan would still be more than eight hundred miles away in Mumbai.

❋ ❋ ❋

A happy reunion at the Minneapolis/St. Paul airport . . .

In what felt like a moment straight out of one of my favorite rom-coms, I ran toward Gavin like I hadn't seen him in years, and when I finally was close enough, I showered him with kisses.

"I'm glad to see you too," Gavin said when we finally pulled away from each other. "So I'm guessing you're glad to be back."

"You don't even know the half of it," I said. "I'm starving. We got anything good at home? Or should we go out somewhere?"

"I think we're pretty much limited to cereal and Hot Pockets," Gavin said with a laugh. "Either of those interest you?"

"How about Thai?" I asked. "I could go for a bowl of red curry."

"Thai it is," Gavin said. "Although I can't believe you passed on the Hot Pockets. I think we even have pepperoni pizza ones."

"Those are pretty hard to resist," I said with a laugh. "But something tells me our Thai food will be a tad more substantial."

Since Gavin had to pick up some gear from Weston's house in St. Paul for an upcoming show, we decided to venture over to the always hoppin' neighborhood of Highland Park, where one of my favorite Thai restaurants is.

My flight had gotten in around three forty-five, so it wasn't even the peak dinner time when we arrived. We were seated immediately—a nice change from Manhattan, where it seems like you have to wait for everything.

After ordering a couple of starters, Gavin and I picked right back up where we'd left off when I went to New York. We talked about my adventures with Lucinda and a few of the new projects he'd been working on, and then Gavin launched into a conversation I can definitely say I never saw coming.

"While you were gone I got to thinking about so many things," he began. "And one of them might surprise you a little."

I didn't know why, but for some reason that statement sounded rather ominous. "Really?" I asked, wondering what in the world he could be referring to. "Have you finally decided to cross over to the dark side and become a Packers fan instead of rooting for the Cowboys?"

"No, nothing that tragic," Gavin said. "You'd know there was something really wrong if I decided to do that."

"I'm glad it's nothing tragic," I said. "So what's going on?"

"I think I'm ready to put my music on the back burner," he said matter-of-factly.

I nearly spit out my spring roll from pure shock.

"That's quite a reaction," Gavin said with a laugh. "What do you think?"

"That's about the last thing I ever expected to hear out of your mouth," I said. "What was it that sparked all of this?"

"You, actually," he said. "And I mean that in the best possible way, Syd. Ever since I've been with you, my angst has disappeared. And frankly, that's what fuels most artists' songs. I've really struggled to write anything that I've been happy with."

Gavin was on a roll, so instead of immediately offering my two cents or telling him how brilliant his songs were, I just listened and let him talk.

"I wish I had the capacity to be happy working as a songwriter for hire, but that's not me either," he said. "I can't crank out stuff that I'm not really jazzed about day in and day out. So I got to thinking about what I'd really like to do, what would really make me feel fulfilled for the long haul. And I think what I'd really like to do is to go to seminary, get my Master of Divinity, and become a pastor."

A sense of relief washed over me. I hadn't been sure what Gavin was going to say, so of course I'd pictured the worst: *So, honey, I've decided that we're going to sell everything we have so we can peddle fruit, veggies, handmade bracelets, and my CDs from our cozy Volkswagen van. Won't it be a great life, unencumbered by the trappings of our materialistic culture?* That actually sounded a bit more like Stinky Nate than Gavin.

"I think that's great, baby," I said reassuringly. "You'd make an excellent pastor. As long as you don't think I'm going to start wearing long prairie dresses with those awful Peter Pan collars."

"What if Prada made prairie dresses with awful Peter Pan collars?" Gavin asked. "Then I bet you'd wear it."

"Well, an ugly couture dress is still an ugly dress," I said. "But if I were forced to wear something hideous, Prada might soften the blow."

"I'll keep that in mind," Gavin said as he munched on Thai wontons. "So you seriously wouldn't mind being married to a minister rather than a rock star?"

"If I recall, I married a hottie named Gavin Williams, not rock star Gavin Williams or Pastor Gavin Williams," I said. "I just want you to do whatever you feel like God's calling you to do."

"Unless it involves living in a Volkswagen van, right?" Gavin asked.

It's funny how often Gavin and I think exactly alike.

"Yes, anything but *that*."

CHAPTER 9

A NEW TAKE ON LADY AND THE TRAMP

A girl likes to be crossed in love now and then. It gives her something to think of . . . and a sort of distinction amongst her companions.

— MR. BENNET (DONALD SUTHERLAND) IN *PRIDE & PREJUDICE*, 2005

EVER SINCE ELI DECIDED to forgive Samantha, he'd felt a new spring in his step. Granted, it had been less than twenty-four hours since he'd made the decision, but it didn't take long before his outlook went from overcast to bright and sunshiny. He actually felt like himself again, which he knew would make everyone who loved him happy too. One person in particular was his sweet, long-suffering mom, who'd constantly worried about him after the breakup and checked in a little too frequently for his liking. He couldn't wait to tell her about the recent development.

And ever since he and Samantha had broken up, he'd gotten out of the habit of going for a run to start the day. As much as he tried to haul his bum out of bed day after day, Eli had convinced himself that he simply didn't have the energy. But all of that changed this morning. As the sun was on the verge of surfacing around five thirty, Eli put on his favorite Nike windpants and a Bethel sweatshirt (with a T-shirt underneath, just in case he got too hot) and laced up his running shoes. He made sure to stretch a little more than usual first. Then off he went.

Eli loved how running almost made him feel like he was weightless. When he was a kid, he'd always dreamed of being an astronaut and what it would be like to float around in space without gravity holding you down. Unfortunately, converting his astronaut dreams to reality required too many science classes for a guy of Eli's talents, which lay more in business. But over the years, Eli had found that running was a suitable alternative. And he didn't even have to put on a space suit or leave the ground to feel like he didn't have a care in the world.

After a long, sweaty run, Eli showered and made his way to the campus center with a bottle of Gatorade (gotta replenish those electrolytes) and the first nonschoolbook he'd read in ages, Brennan Manning's *Ruthless Trust*. His transitional job as an assistant manager at Gap didn't start for a couple of days, so a little R & R was in order.

If someone had told Eli that he'd be working at Gap again, he would've thought they were a little crazy—for lack of a better word. But when he didn't get any nibbles from the first round of résumés he sent out, Eli accepted the job because he'd always done exceptionally well at the task his demanding boss knew he loathed: selling jeans. So when an assistant manager quit, he applied for the position. And when he was offered it, Eli accepted. The pay was decent, and he didn't have to start immediately, so he thought it would be an adequate option until he figured out exactly what he was going to do next, career-wise.

Since finals week was now complete for the majority of the

student body, the campus center was uncharacteristically quiet. Usually it was the epicenter of excitement on campus, the place where gossip about so-and-so was readily available (not that Eli ever listened — ha ha!), the place where couples hung out while sharing a midafternoon snack before their next class began, the place where various organizational meetings took place for the student senate, campus ministries, and so on. But today it was a ghost town, which made it a perfect spot for catching up on a little reading.

But as Eli read a few pages, it didn't take long for company to show up. A group of chatty girls took up residence in the corner table. Hearing them giggle and talk about some guy they'd met at a party, Eli couldn't help but laugh to himself when they described the guy as a "hot little ticket." *Girls. Seriously, they are so hilarious sometimes.*

Eli had rarely met a girl who wasn't boy crazy. And girls at Bethel seemed to be the worst. After they quieted down a little and Eli resumed his reading, a friend sat down at his table. "Hi, Eli," she said. "You look pretty deep in thought, considering it's not a school day."

Eli looked up from his book. It was Elizabeth Embry, his lab partner from his entrepreneurships class. "Elizabeth, hi," Eli said. "No deep thought. Just enjoying a day with nothing on the schedule."

"I know how that goes," Elizabeth said. "I don't start my summer job until next week. Now I don't know what to do with myself. I'm so used to having homework, stuff for the Future Business Leaders club, all that jazz."

"I can't say that I miss it, really," Eli said. "Graduation can't come fast enough for me."

"So what are you going to do now that you've almost got the business degree?" Elizabeth asked. She wondered if she was being too nosy when she noticed the look on Eli's face.

"I'm not sure," he said. "I guess that's what I'm taking the summer to figure out. Everything's changed recently. Sam and I aren't dating anymore—"

"You aren't?" Elizabeth asked. "But I thought you two were serious."

"Apparently we're not now," Eli said with a hint of sarcasm in his voice. "She dumped me for another guy."

"How is that possible?" Elizabeth said sympathetically. "You're one of the sweetest guys I know."

Eli blushed. "Ah, thanks, Liz," he said. "Guess I'm just trying to believe that everything happens for a reason. Maybe there's something I'm supposed to be doing that doesn't involve Sam. Who knows?"

"Whatever you're supposed to do, it'll be great," Elizabeth said, leaning in a little closer to Eli. She had always thought he was cute. But he'd always gone on and on about Sam, so there was no reason to get carried away.

Just as Elizabeth inched closer to Eli, Samantha walked by the campus center and spotted the two of them smiling and looking like they were having a great time together. And even though Samantha had no right to be jealous about the two of them hanging out, she felt an unexpected ache in the pit of her stomach. Eli was already moving on.

Lingering a few seconds longer than she probably should have, Samantha's gaze unexpectedly met Eli's. But instead of a look of pain on his face, she thought he truly looked happy—and at peace. As she turned around and walked away, that hurt her more than seeing Eli with another girl. And again she wondered if she'd made a serious mistake.

✳ ✳ ✳

Getting ready to sign off at KARE-11 . . .

Jane was feeling much, much better today. She'd just wrapped up her morning news show and research for a couple of feature stories that were running sometime next week.

And now that she was feeling better, Jane couldn't seem to wipe a smile off her face. Although she hadn't felt up to going to singles' group the other night (her head still felt the size of a watermelon), Campbell had called. Apparently, his heartfelt message and new commitment to authenticity had gone over well, and it ended up being a great night of sharing and intercessory prayer. After hearing about it, Jane really wished she'd felt better. But apparently her absence seemed to make Campbell's heart grow fonder because he'd called a couple of times since then to "check up" on her.

Now, Jane knew that girls were often quick to jump to conclusions about whether guys liked them or not. She was known to have read too much into things a time or two herself. But Campbell's recent attentiveness made her wonder if that impromptu encounter at Panera was the start of something exciting between them. She'd have to call Sydney to get her opinion. Sydney was always good at giving thoughtful, level-headed advice in situations like these.

✳ ✳ ✳

Chattin' away with Sydney . . .

"So how was New York, Syd?" Samantha asked. She'd just told me she was cooking dinner for Aidan, and I could hear her efforts to tidy up her apartment as we talked.

"Oh, it was fine," I said. "You know with Lucinda, it's never just a business trip. But I did score some new fur-trimmed Manolo Blahnik boots because she said I *had* to have them."

"Don't you have all the luck?" Samantha said with a laugh. "I'm soooo borrowing those."

"Anytime you'd like," I said. "So are you excited about your date tonight?"

"Yes and no," Samantha said. "I'm still deciding what to fix. Any suggestions?"

"How about spaghetti and meatballs, like in *Lady and the Tramp*?" I said sarcastically. "Kind of fitting, don't you think?"

"That's a good one," Samantha said. "A classic pun straight from the Sydney Williams playbook." She paused. "Do you think you're *ever* going to warm up to Aidan?"

"That depends," I began. "If Aidan proves to be someone worth warming up to, I'll reconsider. As of now, he's still in my personal doghouse."

"Suit yourself," Samantha said. "I'm looking forward to proving you wrong. I think people can change."

"Prove away," I said. "I never said that Aidan couldn't change, by the way. All that really matters anyway is that *you're* happy. It doesn't matter what I think."

"We'll see how it goes," Samantha said. "But it's weird. I saw Eli today with some girl I didn't know, and I have to admit, it made me a little jealous. Think that's normal?"

"I think it's a classic case of wanting to have your cake and eat it too," I said. "You want to be with Aidan, not Eli. But if Eli's moving on, you don't necessarily want that either. I think that's pretty normal human behavior. We want it all."

"Ain't that the truth?" Sam said. "I've been thinking a lot lately about what you used to say about prearranged marriages. I think they may be the way to go. Relationships are just too complicated."

I couldn't tell if she was kidding or not. "Trust me, it's all worth it when you find the right guy," I said in my best encouraging tone. "Who knows? Maybe you already have."

"Maybe," she said. "Maybe I have."

"Hey, have you figured out what you're going to do yet after graduation?" I asked.

"Did Mom put you up to this?" Samantha said so quickly I had to laugh.

"No, she didn't. She's definitely brought up the topic," I said. "I was just curious."

"Sorry to get testy," Samantha said. "It's just a sore subject right now with Mom. I did get a couple of interesting offers this week."

"Really?" I said. "Wanna elaborate?"

"I was about to," Samantha said. "I got an acceptance letter from the program at the U of M."

"Sam, that's really exciting!" I said. "Congratulations."

"Thanks," Sam said. "But it's this other letter I got that's really intriguing me at the moment. Arrived completely out of the blue."

"What is it?" I asked curiously. I could hear the change in her voice.

"It's crazy because it's not even something I applied for," Sam began. "One of my professors recommended me for this new program they're offering at Denver Missions Institute. Basically you study so you can become a teacher at the new Christian schools in India."

"India?" I asked cynically. "Is this because Aidan was in India?"

"I know, I know, it probably seems that way," Sam said. "But I'd be in Chennai. If Aidan goes back, he'd be in Mumbai. They aren't even close to each other."

"I stand corrected then," I said. "Sorry for jumping to conclusions."

"It's okay," Samantha said. "I'd think the same thing if I were you. But it does sound like a pretty wonderful opportunity. They said with my grades and GRE scores I'd probably get a good scholarship. So I'm definitely going to see what it's all about."

"I think you should," I offered. "Those are two very exciting offers."

"Yeah," Samantha said. "But I'm going to pray about it, and if you and Gavin would too, that would be helpful."

"Of course, sweetie," I said. "We pray for you already."

"Awww, thanks, Syd," Samantha said. "I guess I'd better start making this dinner. Aidan will be over in a couple of hours."

"Have a good time, Sam. I mean that," I said. "But if he's a jerk even once, you know what to do."

She just laughed. "Talk to you later, sis."

"Bye."

I love my little sister to death, but I often get worked up after a conversation with her. Aidan, Aidan, Aidan! Seriously, what does she see in that guy?

Most people blow off steam by exercising or taking a bubble bath. I do mindless things like playing Scrabulous on Facebook or looking up my favorite actors/actresses on IMDb.com. I'm a full-fledged Internet junkie. Sad, but oh so true.

* * *

The mood is romantic when Aidan arrives . . .

After Syd hung up, Samantha thought again about what her sister had said about Aidan. She promised herself she wouldn't put up with any antics this time—but Aidan hadn't done anything wrong yet, so as far as she was concerned, he was innocent until proven guilty. She just wasn't going to think negative thoughts.

And even though she didn't like the joke behind the *Lady and the Tramp* comment, serving spaghetti and meatballs actually ended up being a pretty good dinner idea. It was simple but tasty and didn't take too long to prepare. Best of all, she didn't have to do extensive grocery shopping to pull it off. All she needed was a great loaf of bread, a couple of garlic cloves . . . and *presto*! dinner was served.

A quick run to the grocery store, a few minutes making meatballs, and a nice store-bought sauce put on simmer did the trick. After she'd pulled a pan of homemade peanut butter chocolate chip cookies (Aidan's favorite) out of the oven, Samantha had just a few minutes to primp before her date.

Promptly at seven o'clock, just as she was glossing her lips, Aidan knocked at the door. *Wow, he's on time. That's new.* She smiled to herself.

Opening the door, she was taken aback by the massive bouquet of pink roses and honeysuckle Aidan held. And he looked hot. "Why hello," Aidan said as he leaned forward and kissed her cheek. "These are for you."

"Thank you so much," Samantha said. "They are absolutely beautiful, Aidan. Come in, come in."

"I wanted to bring something pink."

Sam smiled. "These smell really good. I love them!" She motioned to her Salvation Army couch. "Make yourself at home. I'm going to put these in a vase."

Aidan kept himself occupied by looking at the photos on top of her bookshelf. There were framed snapshots of Sam and Sydney in a variety of places: New York, their hometown in Wisconsin, downtown Minneapolis. Mixed in were several shots of her with her college friends. In some Samantha was dressed to the nines. In others she was more laid-back and casual in sweats or jeans and a T-shirt. In his humble opinion, Samantha looked great in anything she wore.

But one particular picture, one of Samantha and Eli from the recent costume ball at Bethel, made Aidan's stomach turn. *Why does she still have that?*

Not far from it, there was another shot of Samantha and Eli at a Twins game. They were each holding a huge inflatable baseball bat and grinning from ear to ear. They definitely had the look of a couple in love. Why were these photos still on display?

Aidan knew that he and Samantha were still just figuring things out; it was too soon to say they were even in a relationship. But how much of a chance did they have if Samantha still had pictures of her and Eli out in plain view?

"Hope you're hungry because I've got quite the feast prepared," Samantha called out from the kitchen. "Ready to eat?"

"I'm starving," Aidan said. And he added, "Nice pictures, by the way." He walked into the kitchen.

"Thanks," Samantha said. "Haven't you seen those before?"

"Not . . . *all* of them," Aidan replied, hoping Samantha would take the bait.

But she didn't. "Hope you still like pasta," she said.

"*Mmmm*," Aidan said. "Mind if I serve you?"

"Not at all," Samantha said. "But just a small amount of sauce for me, please. My tummy doesn't like all the acid."

"I remember," Aidan said softly. He scooped up a generous portion of noodles and added just a touch of sauce to the center, along with the meatballs.

"Thanks," Samantha said, taking the plate from him. "I've been meaning to ask you about that bracelet you're wearing. It's very interesting."

"Yeah, a few of the kids from the orphanage made it for me and made me promise I'd never take it off," Aidan said. "So I won't—unless it literally rots off my arm."

"Rots, huh? Nice imagery," Samantha said with a laugh. "I think it's sweet—very colorful."

"I love it. One of the little girls, Aadab, couldn't wait to give it to me," Aidan said. "Her name means 'hope and need,' which I think is fitting. Every time I see that bracelet on my wrist, I think about those kids. If my time in India makes any difference in their lives, I would be thrilled beyond belief. As difficult as life is there, the experience is . . . amazing."

"I can only imagine," Samantha said. "I'm really happy you decided to go."

"You were the one who inspired me," Aidan said, taking her hand. "Mind if I bless the food?"

"No, go ahead," Samantha said.

"Dear God, thank you so much for this day and for this delicious meal. Bless the hands that prepared it, Lord, and our conversation this evening. In Jesus' name, Amen."

"Thanks so much for praying, Aidan," Samantha began. "But how can you thank God for a delicious meal you haven't tasted yet?"

"Good point," Aidan said. "Guess I have faith in the cook."

CHAPTER 10

MEDDLING FOR MONEY: A NEW WAY TO PLAY CUPID

I know you can be overwhelmed, and you can be underwhelmed, but can you ever just be whelmed?

— CHASTITY (GABRIELLE UNION) IN *10 THINGS I HATE ABOUT YOU,* 1999

IF SOMEONE ASKED ME to write them all down, I could probably come up with at least a hundred reasons why life as a freelance writer is great. And sleeping in until ten thirty this morning was definitely one of them.

When I worked at *Get Away*, the day promptly started at eight thirty, whether I wanted it to or not. Now, save for the rare before-ten client meeting, my schedule is entirely my own. Well, as long as I meet my assigned deadlines. That's never been too much of a problem, so I can basically work when I need to — at the crack of dawn, if I feel so inspired, or late at night with Jay Leno and Conan O'Brien to keep me company.

Although Gavin and I skipped the late-night talk shows last night, we stayed up and talked until close to three a.m. Continuing our conversation from dinner, we wrote down a list of seminaries that would be the best options for a Master of Divinity program, discussed how we felt about moving out of Minneapolis so he could pursue academic life, and talked about what that ultimately meant for his musical career. Would Gavin continue to write for aspiring artists? Or would he temporarily quit music and pick up his guitar only when he felt a creative impulse? He still wasn't sure, but he was leaning toward the cold turkey approach for the time being.

Like any good brainstorming session, we didn't come up with any hard and fast answers—just a lot of good ideas to ponder and pray about. While it was definitely an unexpected turn of events for me—I thought Gavin would always be a musician—the proud wife in me couldn't have been more thrilled that Gavin wasn't content to settle for status quo in his life or career. And if becoming a pastor was what fulfilled him professionally and spiritually, I was 100 percent onboard.

Thanks to Lucinda's last-minute advertorial project, though, I didn't have much time to give it any more thought. Gavin was planning to get in touch with a few seminaries today to see what options would be available for the fall, so there would be an update later. Given that it was May thirtieth, a little late to be submitting applications, we didn't know how many viable options there would be, but we would know soon.

Meanwhile, I needed to start writing copy for the fashion houses that had bought advertising in the issue Lucinda needed to rework. Gwen Stefani's L.A.M.B. perfume and clothing line (it's an acronym for Love. Angel. Music. Baby.) was first on the list. Then Prada, Jimmy Choo, Dolce & Gabbana, Dooney & Bourke . . . and the list went on and on. It was going to be a long day.

＊　＊　＊

Deep thoughts while cleaning her kitchen . . .

Although Samantha could've slept in (she had no place to be, after all), she was wide awake by seven. Considering that normally she was barely functional at this hour (without her morning coffee), it meant only one thing: Samantha had a lot on her mind.

Seeing Eli yesterday had shifted her emotions into overdrive. She didn't like seeing him with another girl. Worse, she didn't like facing the possibility that Eli might have already gotten over her. Was that unreasonably possessive and downright silly considering she'd ended things? Absolutely. But that peaceful look on Eli's face haunted her somehow. And because of that, Samantha doubted her own sanity with relationships yet again.

As she cleaned up the remnants of last night's spaghetti dinner and loaded the dishwasher, Samantha thought that somehow those uncertain feelings about Eli had crept into her date with Aidan last night. Oh, she and Aidan had had a perfectly good time. Aidan's prayer before dinner was thoughtful and sweet. And Samantha thought it was so endearing that he was wearing the bracelet from the kids at the orphanage. Their conversation during dinner was pleasant enough too. No red flags. He endlessly complimented the dinner she'd made. And he was excited when Samantha told him she was considering studying at Denver Missions Institute to prepare for a career as a teacher in India.

But for one reason or another, Samantha felt blasé about the evening with Aidan. She'd really believed she wanted a second chance with him, and she'd sacrificed what she had with Eli to do it. But . . . she wasn't feeling it.

She had dreamed about a new start with Aidan time and again and had wondered if a second chance was all it was cracked up to be. Now that she had it, even with all the positive changes Aidan had made in his life, she wasn't completely sure that's what she wanted. What was causing these feelings of uncertainty? Was it Eli? Was it Aidan? Or was it the pressure of her college career wrapping up? Was it the necessity of making major decisions about her future that was causing everything to spin out of control? There were so many questions that needed answering. Samantha was thankful that she didn't start her summer job until Monday. A good long weekend was exactly what she needed to figure a few things out.

* * *

Typing away at my desk . . .

Rachel McAdams' manager told me that her interview was going to have to be via e-mail—she was in the middle of filming a movie and didn't have any spare time for a phone interview—so I was a little nervous about delivering that particular news to Lucinda. Being the results-oriented person she was, Lucinda always told me to make the impossible possible, no matter how impossible the task was.

But with the deadline looming for the advertorial, Lucinda was more sympathetic than usual because she was under the gun. "You're saving my rear end," she said. "Don't worry about it. Just make the content as compelling as you can." Now *that* I could do.

While I was thinking of clever questions to zip over to Rachel's publicist in the next ten minutes, I was distracted by an e-mail with a subject line that definitely caught my attention: "Are you the new Lucy for the Lovelorn columnist?"

> From: Nick Taylor nicktaylor79@gotmail.com
> To: Sydney Williams <sydneyawilliams@gotmail.com>
> Subject: Are you the new Lucy for the Lovelorn columnist?
>
> Hey Sydney,
>
> Hope you're doing well. Just wanted to thank you again for the great interview. The band can't wait to see the story in print! Also wanted to let you know that my cousin Lucy (the one I was telling you about who writes the advice column you like) is expecting a baby and is planning to temporarily give up her duties as of next month.
>
> Since you mentioned how much you enjoy the column and that you are a bit of a matchmaker yourself, I took the liberty of mentioning you as a possible replacement. So I thought I'd give you a heads-up in case she calls. Hope that was okay.
>
> Enjoy your weekend,
> Nick

Wow, what an exciting development. I would *love* to be the new "Lucy for the Lovelorn" columnist. Not only would it be a whole lot of fun, but I would be syndicated. That's any writer's dream. (Well, that and winning a Pulitzer.) And since I haven't had much time to work on my magnum opus, I'd be happy to settle for the former, if it could be worked out. Too excited not to respond right away, I clicked reply and tried to play it as cool as I could.

From: Sydney Williams sydneyawilliams@gotmail.com
To: Nick Taylor <nicktaylor79@gotmail.com>
Subject: Re: Are you the new Lucy for the Lovelorn columnist?

Hey Nick,

It was great to hear from you. I had a lot of fun at the interview too and look forward to writing the story. My deadline is in a couple of weeks, so before long, the story will be off to the printer and ready for the band to check out. Yee-haw!

Thank you so much for thinking of me for "Lucy for the Lovelorn." You're right, that's something I would love to do, so I definitely hope to hear from Lucy soon. It wouldn't be an easy task filling her shoes, but I'm always up for a challenge.

Hope you have a great weekend too.

Peace,
Sydney

After hitting send, I resumed my advertorial writing with a big smile on my face. *Sydney Williams as "Lucy for the Lovelorn."* I definitely liked the sound of that.

❋ ❋ ❋

Samantha picks up her phone for some sound advice . . .

Sydney's work schedule was pretty intense most of the time, so Samantha knew she was probably in the middle of a writing project—but she decided to chance it and give her a call anyway. Samantha was really feeling down about her Eli/Aidan conundrum and was beginning to regret the decision she'd made to break up with Eli.

Samantha knew that what was done was done, and a phone call with her straight-shooting sister probably wouldn't make any difference. But she still hoped that Sydney would give her some much-needed affirmation. Something like, "You're totally doing the right thing pursuing this with Aidan, just give it time, *blah, blah, blah . . .*" If she were truly honest with herself, though, she knew her decision had been a little impetuous. But even Sydney, who had been equally adventurous in life and love, had told her that she should give it a try with Aidan. Hadn't she?

Okay, that's it, Samantha thought. *I'm going to quit wallowing over Eli and give this relationship with Aidan my all. If it doesn't work out, well, I've given it my best effort.*

And with that sense of resolve, Samantha slammed her cell phone shut. She didn't need to bother Sydney; she just needed to give it more time.

* * *

Sydney's got a new gig . . .

Like most people, I would say Friday is easily my favorite day of the workweek. But this Friday had been especially exciting, given all the new developments. Not long after Nick sent me the e-mail about his cousin Lucy, Lucy herself called to interview me as a potential ghostwriter; her editor trusted her decision implicitly.

You know how you just click immediately with some people? Well, that was Lucy and me. Not only did we have many of the same superficial interests, like favorite TV shows and movies, but we shared many of the same perspectives on romantic relationships and a sarcastic sense of humor to boot. But the deal for the "Lucy for the Lovelorn" column wasn't officially sealed until she'd reviewed a few of my writing samples, then called me back and read me a couple of selected reader letters over the phone and asked me to respond with my best off-the-cuff advice.

One case involved cheating and another was a "Do you think he likes me or not?" scenario. Apparently I passed with flying colors because Lucy offered me the job on the spot.

"Right now, I see this as a temporary gig," Lucy said. "All depends on what happens when the baby comes. But as of now, you're me if you want to be."

I didn't blink an eye. "So when do I start?"

"How about next week?" she asked. "I'm getting bigger and crankier every day; my husband wouldn't mind if you started tomorrow."

"Of course," I said. "Next week it is."

"Perfect!" Lucy said. "I'll just have all the 'Lucy' mail forwarded to you."

"Sounds like a plan." And we said good-bye.

After Lucy and I hung up, I couldn't wait to call Gavin. So I saved all the documents I'd been working on and called to tell him his wife was going to be syndicated.

"Sydney! That is so incredible," Gavin said. "But I guess I'm not really all that surprised. I always thought you'd be syndicated someday."

"Thank you for that vote of confidence, honey," I said with a hearty laugh. "Now I'm going to get paid to give out love advice. How cool is that?"

"You're going to have to be careful," Gavin said soberly. "One piece of bad advice, and those hate letters will start coming."

"I sure hope not," I said. "I don't know how I'd handle that."

"That's why I'm here," Gavin said confidently. "To protect my wife from those crazy lovelorn types."

"That's a relief," I said. "I hadn't thought of any potential backlash."

"Of course not," Gavin said. "You're the eternal optimist — just one of the many things I love about you."

"Awww," I replied. "You're the sweetest."

Gavin then informed me that a celebration was in order. Since reservations aren't always easy to score at the last minute on a Friday night (even in Minneapolis), we decided on the next best thing: thick, yummy, cheesy pizza at one of the first places we ever ate together when we started dating.

It was crowded, like probably every restaurant was in downtown Minneapolis at this hour, but we secured a corner table and perused the menu. Feeling adventurous, we shied away from ordering our usual — The Classic with all the standard pizza ingredients — and decided to try the much-talked-about Baked Potato Pizza with buttery garlic mashed potatoes, broccoli, tomatoes, cheddar cheese, and bacon. As we waited, I grabbed Gavin's hand and said, "I told you all about my day — so how was yours, honey?"

"It was really productive," he said. "After a songwriting session with Jaguar, I called a few seminaries to request information. Turns out it's not too late to apply to a few of them, including Vanderbilt in Nashville."

"Really?" I asked. "That's great news! I've heard that Vanderbilt has a great divinity school. You thinking of applying?"

"What would you think about living there?" Gavin asked.

"There's definitely worse places to live," I said with a laugh. "And professionally, it wouldn't be bad either. A lot of my clients are in Nashville."

"You don't sound entirely convinced," Gavin said. "Granted, it would be a little strange for me too. Especially since I wouldn't be doing music . . . in Music City. But it could be a really good opportunity—educationally speaking."

"Definitely," I said, stroking his arm. "I'm not opposed to moving to Nashville. I just need to process it."

"Of course," Gavin said as he grabbed my hand. "I'd expect nothing less from my darling, opinionated wife. That's just one option, though. There's also some great seminaries here."

"Wherever you think has the best program," I said. "I'm not handcuffed to staying here. Fortunately, my job is portable."

"And that's a blessing," Gavin said as the server delivered our pizza to the table. "In honor of your new column, you get the first piece."

As Gavin served me up a slice of the specialty pizza, I silently thanked God for such an incredible husband. I simply couldn't imagine life without him.

*Back in New York, Lucinda gets ready for a first date to
    remember . . .*

Like any woman about to go out with a complete stranger, Lucinda
had a major case of the butterflies in anticipation of meeting
Philip. It wasn't like she had particularly high expectations for
the date. After all, she was forced to rely on Sydney's fairly rough
sketch of him and had no idea what he really looked like. But
the e-mails they'd exchanged over the past few days proved that
Philip was witty—always a good quality.

Since Lucinda made it a habit to always look her best (working
in fashion, there was always someone silently—or sometimes not
so silently—critiquing her ensembles), her attire certainly didn't
disappoint for her blind date. Opting for a chic, sophisticated
look that wasn't binding for a change (a rarity for a fashionista
like herself), Lucinda sported a black and pink silk Diane von
Fürstenberg wrap dress (they were so flattering that even if you
scarfed down a Krispy Kreme for breakfast, you still looked fab),
sky-high black Manolo Blahnik heels that she'd bought when
Sydney was in town (with decidedly uncool but comfy insoles to
keep her feet from blistering), and simple silver drop earrings that
looked perfect with her hair pinned in a messy updo. To match
the laid-back but slightly dressy vibe, Lucinda went the minimalist
route with her makeup, favoring a nude color palette to accentuate
her eyes, cheeks, and lips. With a quick flick of DiorShow mascara
to make her mile-long lashes look even longer, Lucinda was ready.

Philip had suggested meeting for martinis at a pub near his
house, and then they'd head to dinner afterward. The fact that
he'd make dinner reservations in advance (a must on a Friday night
in Manhattan) and was so secretive about where he was taking

her really intrigued Lucinda. Maybe—just maybe—Sydney had actually picked out a real Prince Charming for her and this was the first of many exciting dates together. Lucinda usually made fun of people who embraced what she cynically believed was a silly, storybook view of romance, but if she was honest with herself, she wanted what every other girl wanted too. Flowers. Valentines. Kisses that actually meant something. Long walks on the beach. But Lucinda knew she shouldn't get carried away; this was only a first date.

Giving herself one last glance in her mirror, Lucinda locked the front door, hailed a cab, and headed to the pub to meet her mystery man. Oh, the excitement!

* * *

Apparently, guys get first-date jitters too . . .

Normally, the dating rulebook wouldn't suggest picking the crème de la crème of restaurants for a first date. But for a classy woman like Lucinda, Philip didn't want to spare any expense, so he'd chosen one of his favorite romantic spots: One if by Land on Barrow Street. And since he wanted the restaurant he was taking her to to be a surprise, he thought a drink beforehand would be a nice way to break the ice and meet each other for the first time.

Now it was just a few minutes before Philip needed to be at the pub to meet Lucinda, and he was battling a serious wave of nausea in the taxi on the way there. *What if she doesn't like me?* Philip thought as he tied the laces to his black Hugo Boss shoes. *Or worse yet, what if she gets bored with me?*

Philip hadn't had the best track record with women. He was

married very briefly (just over a month) to his college sweetheart, Isabella, before she left him for her chiropractor. And then there was Anna, to whom he was briefly engaged a few years later. Only a month and a half after Philip had sprung for the two-carat engagement ring she'd wanted from Tiffany's, Anna started seeing her allergist. It had taken a couple of years in counseling for him to learn not to take rejection so personally.

Since then, Philip hadn't dated anyone seriously, just a few dinner dates here and there. He knew he was a nice guy, so it was kind of depressing. And while he'd never be mistaken for a fashion model, Philip was relatively good-looking and well-dressed. He paid extra money for good haircuts at a trendy salon and wasn't afraid of regular manicures or using grooming products. Smart and successful, even a homeowner, Philip also knew how to treat a girl right (thanks to his mama, a proper Southern lady), but all the women he got involved with ended up leaving anyway. It was as if being a good guy wasn't enough. There had to be some element of danger in the relationship to keep things going.

Why did girls always like the bad guys? What was their mystique, anyway? A mutual friend of Philip and Anna's had told Philip that Anna had gotten pregnant with Dr. Allergist's baby, and he promptly gave her the heave-ho. And Isabella, well, he never heard what happened with her and the chiropractor, but he hoped she was happy—whoever she was with.

Despite his less than stellar relationships, Philip still held out hope that the right girl was out there. When he'd spotted Sydney at the bagel shop, he thought maybe . . . Of course, she turned out to be married. But when she'd offered Lucinda as a suitable alternative, well, that really excited him. And now here he was, about to go on a date with her. Who knew? Maybe the third time would be the charm.

* * *

Lucinda and Philip finally meet . . .

Lucinda arrived at the pub first and didn't spot anyone who fit Philip's description. *Is he gonna stand me up? That would be just my luck.*

But just as Lucinda was about to embark on a premature pity party for herself, in walked a guy who had to be him. And he didn't disappoint — Philip was looking very fetching in a navy blue pinstriped blazer, a white-collared shirt (Lucinda guessed it was Polo), a great pair of dressy jeans, and black lace-up dress shoes.

She walked toward him, and Philip smiled as he greeted her with a kiss on the cheek. "You must be Lucinda."

"Guilty as charged," she replied, returning his smile.

"I must say you're very pretty," Philip said. "Want to sit down and grab a drink?"

"Well, that's the general — " But rather than resorting to a sarcastic remark, Lucinda paused briefly, then corrected herself. "I would, thank you," she said, proud of how she'd maintained her composure and hadn't said the first thing that came out of her mouth like she usually did. Maybe she could turn a new leaf.

After finding a couple of empty spots at the bar, Philip pulled out a chair for Lucinda.

"Why, thank you," Lucinda purred. "I love a man with good manners. Did you grow up down South or something?"

"Yes, ma'am," Philip said. "I grew up in Knoxville, Tennessee." If she listened carefully, she could hear traces of a Southern accent.

"Did you like it there?" Lucinda asked. "I grew up in Milledgeville, Georgia, and I couldn't wait to get out. I always aspired to be a New York girl."

"When was I growing up, I didn't know any better," Philip said. "I thought Knoxville was the best place in the whole wide world."

"That's really great," Lucinda said. "I was always convinced that I'd been switched at birth with some poor girl in New York. She hated the theater and public transportation and didn't understand why her family couldn't have a nice porch swing. And there I was, eating grits for breakfast and just dying to be in a creative, fast-paced place like New York. Clearly, if our mothers had been given the correct baby, everything would've turned out swimmingly."

"My, my, you've got quite a vivid imagination!" Philip said with a laugh. "I used to think I was switched at birth too — because everyone in my family has blond hair and blue eyes except me."

"I happen to like hazel eyes and dark hair far better, so you're in luck." Lucinda smiled.

"Okay, so maybe I wasn't born into the wrong family after all," Philip said. "Maybe I've just never met the, um, right girl." And as they continued their conversation, Philip's nerves finally calmed down, allowing him to truly enjoy his evening out with Lucinda.

After a round of drinks and plenty of great get-to-know-you conversation, Philip and Lucinda hailed a cab and made their way to the restaurant. "So where are we going?" Lucinda asked. "The suspense is killing me."

"What are some of your favorite foods?" Philip asked.

"I don't cook, so it's usually sushi," Lucinda said sheepishly, thinking Philip was probably one of those guys who liked his women to cook.

"Unfortunately we're not having sushi," Philip said. "One of my favorite places is called One if by Land, so I thought I'd take you there."

"You're kidding," Lucinda squealed. "Something's always come up to prevent me from actually eating there, even though I've planned to a few times. I'm so excited."

"I'm glad," Philip said. "Their cheese course and Gruyère gnocchi is to die for. Not to mention the dessert menu. The food is so good it makes me want to quit my day job and become a food critic just so I could give them a five-star review."

"So . . . what *is* your day job?" Lucinda asked.

Philip reminded himself that not every woman was obsessed with money the way Anna had been. *Quit being paranoid*, he thought.

"I'm a business owner, actually," Philip said.

"Anything I've heard of?"

"Depends if you're a fan of Pinkberry frozen yogurt," Philip said. "I own three shops in Manhattan."

"Get out of town!" Lucinda said. "I'm a Pinkberry fanatic. It's one of the few guilt-free desserts I let myself enjoy."

"That's great," Philip said. "It's always fun watching the lines snake out the door—who knew frozen yogurt could become an addiction?"

"I've always maintained that the Pinkberry people put an addictive substance in the yogurt so I'll crave it every day." Lucinda laughed.

"Not a bad theory!" Philip laughed with her. "I *have* to have the green tea with mangos a couple of times a week."

"Mmm. I've never tried that combination," Lucinda said.

"You'll have to let me treat you sometime," Philip said, surprised by his stroke of confidence.

"I just might have to take you up on that," Lucinda said. "You know — after we see how it goes."

Philip liked Lucinda's spunk. She definitely wasn't the sort of wilting-flower type he was used to dating. She would keep him on his toes for sure.

A few minutes later, they were seated in the dimly lit quarters of One if by Land. It was truly breathtaking, romantically decorated with red roses and candlelight. Lucinda thought if the food was even half as good as the atmosphere, the blind date would be worth it. Besides, it seemed to be going very, very well.

"So when you're not working, what's your favorite way to let off steam?" Philip asked, trying to keep the conversation light and interesting, while picking up important information along the way.

"I'm afraid you're not going to like this," Lucinda said, trying out a line she always used to determine if her dates had 'til-death-do-us-part potential (or even qualified as potentially long-term). "Shopping usually does the trick for me. Or a hydrating facial." She gave him a sideways look.

While it might have seemed a touch manipulative as a method for weeding out dates, Lucinda found these tactics necessary. She'd been briefly engaged five years ago, and her fiancé hadn't bothered to tell her until a month before the wedding that she'd be on a strict budget that didn't include any "unnecessary shopping trips." Perish the thought! To add insult to injury, his definition of what she *had* to have was quite different from hers. A Miu Miu skirt spotted in the Bloomingdale's window during her lunch break at work constituted "necessary" to Lucinda; to her tightwad fiancé, a Miu Miu skirt, no matter how adorable, fell under the category of a superfluous extravagance. Toothpaste, face cream, a pair of running shoes once a year—those were necessary. Needless to say, when Lucinda discovered this, she couldn't marry him. She knew now that this was something she should've discovered and discussed much earlier in the relationship. But better late than never, right?

Philip didn't even flinch when Lucinda mentioned her love of shopping. "There's nothing quite like retail therapy, is there?" he said. "We probably don't shop for the same stuff, though."

Awww, he used the words *retail therapy*. That definitely warmed Lucinda's heart.

"What do you shop for?" Lucinda said. "I stick with the stereotypical girl things. Clothes. Makeup. Shoes. Bags."

"I bought a new car once," Philip said sheepishly. "But that was unusual, and I took it back. I've had a trusty BMW for over five years."

A BMW, huh? Well, if you're not going to get a new car for five years, that's definitely not a bad way to go.

"It could be worse, right?" Lucinda joked. "It could be a trusty Geo."

"That would be tragic," Philip agreed. "Although it might be a better choice, given the traffic situation."

"So other than a car, what does your retail therapy look like?" Lucinda asked. "Golf clubs? DVDs? Electronics?"

Philip laughed. "Electronics are totally my weakness," he said. "I waited in line for close to twenty hours for my iPhone."

"I wouldn't wait that long for a Chanel sample sale!" Lucinda teased. "And it's *Chanel* we're talking about here."

Before Lucinda had time to explain what a sample sale was, their food arrived. And my, it looked delectable.

✳ ✳ ✳

Back from the gym, Aidan is reflective . . .

Most people wouldn't exactly feel contemplative after a long workout, but that's what Aidan was feeling as he cooled down tonight. Samantha, of course, was the reason. Overall, he was really enjoying her. Just having her back in his life felt like a miracle—something he didn't really deserve, and he knew it.

But as much fun as Aidan was having, he couldn't escape the nagging feeling that Samantha was holding back a little. When he tried to kiss her the other night, just to thank her for dinner, she turned her head, and he ended up bumping her neck instead. Embarrassing, to say the least.

Was she still thinking of Eli? Was she regretting the decision she'd made to pursue things with Aidan? He needed to get to the bottom of it, sooner rather than later.

✳ ✳ ✳

Walking through Central Park on a perfect night . . .

Dinner had tasted just as great as it looked—not always an easy task for a chef to accomplish. The quail was perfectly cooked, each bite tender and buttery—truly a delicacy. Lucinda could've just eaten the quail, but the exotic cheese plate and red potatoes with truffles were impossible to resist. And as if dinner wasn't sinful enough, Philip fed her bite after bite of the vanilla bean crème brûlée, which made her thankful she'd worn a dress that stretched with her. If she'd worn her skinny jeans, she would've been in serious trouble.

After dinner, Philip suggested a walk in Central Park, an invitation Lucinda accepted without hesitation. It was the perfect night to be in Central Park—there was a light breeze, the stars were out, and she and Philip hadn't yet run out of things to talk about. Whew!

All in all, the night had truly been a success, which thoroughly surprised Lucinda. After a slew of bad boyfriends and lackluster dates over the years, she'd trained herself to keep her expectations low. Then when someone good (like Philip!) came along, she was pleasantly surprised. Of course, she always hoped her dates would go well, but her self-preservation techniques kept the pain at bay when they didn't.

But whatever ended up happening with Philip in the future, they'd had the perfect date tonight, which was more than enough to make Lucinda happy for now.

Oh, wait . . . Philip leaned in for a kiss. And as his soft lips met Lucinda's, the perfect date now had the perfect fairy tale ending. Life was indeed looking up (at last!) for Ms. Lucinda A. Buffington. *Thank you, Sydney!*

CHAPTER 11

BOTTOM LINE? LOVE AIN'T EASY

I want to see what love looks like when it's triumphant. I
haven't had a good laugh in a week.

—PETER WARNE (CLARK GABLE) IN *IT HAPPENED ONE NIGHT*, 1934

Fast-forward three months . . .

WHEN LUCY TOLD ME I'd be receiving a mammoth amount of
letters from readers of the "Lucy for the Lovelorn" column,
she wasn't kidding. Ever since I'd taken over her duties, my mail-
box had been overflowing with questions about the mysteries and
complexities of the opposite sex.

The letters I received were interesting—and that's putting it
mildly. Some were garden-variety "Do you think he likes me or
not?" sort of questions, while others were downright scary in the
"Every breath you take, every move you make, I'll be watching
you" kind of way. Do you think Sting . . . ? Nah.

Sometimes I felt grossly unqualified and uncomfortable
reading, let alone answering, those types of questions in print. So
rather than encouraging people in print to get the restraining order
they really needed, I'd send a letter back with recommendations
for licensed professionals they could talk to. I felt guilty leaving

even one person like this hanging for any period of time, so I tried to respond as soon as humanly possible.

When you have a slew of other clients to take care of, being Lucy isn't always easy, that's for sure. I chose only two letters each week to answer in the column, but wading through all the mail I got felt like a full-time job in itself. Not that I was complaining. I mean, the gig paid great and allowed me to be published in a number of national newspapers as a ghostwriter. And the letters I received when I provided helpful advice made the whole experience rewarding. Really, they did. But take this letter, for example. Aren't some things just common sense? Does a person really need an advice columnist to answer a question like this?

> *Dear Lucy for the Lovelorn,*
> *My boyfriend of six months seems to be breaking*
> *out and sneezing every time my cat, Scrawny, is*
> *nearby. Because of the unpleasant nature of the*
> *symptoms, my b/f wants me to get rid of Scrawny.*
> *The trouble is I've had Scrawny for six years, and*
> *I've only known this guy for six months. So do I*
> *say good-bye to my cat to make this relationship*
> *work, or do I hold my ground?*
> *Thanks for your help,*
> *Marsha, Sacramento, California*

> *Darling Marsha,*
> *The answer to the question depends on the quality*
> *of said boyfriend. If you care about this guy and*
> *envision being the mother of his children one*

*day, you'll find a suitable home for Scrawny. If
not, well, at least you'll get to spend your Friday
nights with Scrawny as you find the company of a
nonallergic boyfriend in the meantime.*

Love,
Lucy

Then, some letters like this one really broke my heart.

Dear Lucy for the Lovelorn,
*I've never written to a love columnist before, but I
was hoping you could help. No matter what I do,
I never have any luck getting a date. I've asked
lots of girls out before, but they just say no. Is God
playing a cruel joke on me? Is there someone out
there for me? Do you have any advice for a guy
like me?*

Asher, Augusta, Maine

Darling Asher,
*I wish I could say I had all the answers to your
questions, but alas, I'm a mere mortal who
happens to dole out relationship advice for part of
her living. But I will say this: You're making an
effort, and that's an important step in the right
direction. Some people just wait around for Mr. or
Ms. Right to show up at their front door. Others,
like you, are brave enough to actually put your
heart out there on the line. So all I can say is keep*

*trying and make sure the girls you are asking out
are actually worth your time. Because if you're as
sweet as you sound in your letter, you'll definitely
meet someone — it's just a matter of time.*

    Love,
    Lucy
*PS I don't think God ever plays cruel jokes on
people. Only camels. I mean, c'mon, humps? What
are those about?*

This week, however, I was pretty sure one of my own friends
had sought my help through "Lucy." Although her moniker was
Laci in the letter, it sounded an awful lot like Jane, who was rather
frustrated with me and Campbell at the moment. Here's what
Laci had to say:

Dear Lucy,
*I've been a faithful reader of your column for
a few months now* [hmmm, that's right about
when I started, my first clue that it was Jane],
*and I've always been impressed with your wit and
wisdom in matters of the heart* [awww — thanks,
Jane].

    Now that I've buttered you up [and you
certainly have, Jane], *I have a small matter
that I'd like your thoughts on. A friend of mine,
a very good friend, suggested that my landlord
and I would really hit it off* [landlord — wink,
wink]. *And I believe that we have. We've shared
meals together. We've hung out in group settings.*

We've chatted at length and even shared extremely
personal things with each other. There's been all
kinds of flirty banter and furtive glances but not
one date, aside from a lunch together when I was
sick [hmmm, I seem to remember that].

I've been hoping and pining for a few months
now, and I'm wondering whether to just come
out and say something to him. I know I'm being
a tad impatient, but I really, really want to see if
this could go anywhere. Even worse, I find myself
getting increasingly more angry with the friend
who suggested it in the first place. I know it's not
fair, but this thing is driving me crazy. I can't even
talk to her. I know he's in a rough spot, being my
landlord and all, but I think a dating relationship
could work if he's willing to give it a try.

What should I do? Any help would be mucho
appreciated.

Laci, Minneapolis, Minnesota

I couldn't resist using Laci's letter in the column this week
and wondered if things between Jane and I would be a little less
tense if she read Lucy's advice. I sure hoped it would do the trick
because I really missed talking to Jane. She hadn't called me in two
weeks, and in an e-mail last week, she chalked it up to "chronic
busyness." But now I knew better. And it made me wonder if she
knew that I knew the letter was from her. It was all unsettling,
but in the meantime, I let Laci know what Lucy thought about
her dilemma.

149

Darling Laci,
Thank you for your kind words about the
column—that means a lot! I'm hoping that even
if my advice turns out to be a lemon you'll still
keep reading because, frankly, I need the readers.

But in all seriousness, I think you should
say something to your landlord if you feel that
strongly about him. If you're sure he's flirting
(and trust me, it's so easy to misinterpret a guy's
intentions—they are truly confusing creatures
sometimes) and you've had a good time together in
the past, it seems worth the risk. And hey, if you
chicken out, you can always cut out this column
and tape it to his door (in a sealed envelope, of
course, so the other tenants don't see) with a note
from you that says, "So what do you think?"

Or you can keep quiet and continue to live an
existence plagued by feelings for a man who may
or may not know how you feel. Ultimately, it's
your choice. Make the best one for you.
Love,
Lucy

I wasn't sure what would happen between Jane and Campbell if she did end up saying something, but I hoped that she and I would start talking again sooner rather than later. I hated the idea that one suggestion I made might have messed up our friendship in any way. I hoped and prayed that a resolution would come soon.

❋ ❋ ❋

Golden Gate Park, here they come!

After prayer, much deliberation, and the wise counsel of friends and family on whether to go to grad school or move to Denver to pursue the missions opportunity, Samantha opted for neither. For now, anyway.

"A decision like that is just too big to be made so quickly," her pastor had told her. "You need to take some time to really decide what's best for you."

Even her mom, who'd hounded her constantly about her future plans, believed she was making the best decision. "Maybe you just need to work for a while, earn some money, then figure it out," she'd said. "And you know you have my complete support, whatever you do."

That was a relief—a huge relief—because Samantha was most afraid of disappointing her mom. She'd spent all that money sending Sam to college, and Sam had yet to select a clear-cut career path. But Samantha also knew that it was far too important a decision to take lightly, so she continued to seek God's direction for the next step in her life.

And finally, after some initial weirdness getting reacquainted and working through a few trust issues, Samantha and Aidan's relationship was going strong. They'd been enjoying their time together so much, in fact, that Aidan suggested a minivacation together over Labor Day weekend. It would be Sam's choice.

After careful deliberation and a quick check of airfare rates, Samantha had decided on San Francisco. She'd done her fair share of traveling in her college years, but she'd never been to California and thought it was high time. Sydney was a big fan of Los Angeles and highly recommended it for an enjoyable weekend away, but

Samantha thought San Francisco might strike a more romantic note. Golden Gate Park. Ghirardelli Square. The Golden Gate Bridge. Alcatraz. Cable cars. That wonderful sourdough bread, a San Francisco tradition. Samantha couldn't wait to experience it all with Aidan by her side.

As strange as it sounded, Samantha was convinced that the pain she experienced with Aidan the first time had made her a better girlfriend this time. She'd learned to stand up for herself and not let her crush on Aidan overshadow pressing issues that would arise from time to time. She'd also learned to make time for herself and not let the relationship supersede other facets of her life, particularly her time with God.

The last time Samantha dated Aidan, her life was so consumed by everything happening with them that other parts of her life, especially the spiritual part, suffered. Now with a second chance at making their relationship work, they were making time to pray together (not just at meals) and had been reading through a couples' devotional. Much like her opinionated older sister, Samantha usually found books like those cheesy—and about as relevant as a cassette player is these days. But it turned out this book had sparked some great discussions between her and Aidan, especially when it came to what life might look like in the future.

As they got to talking, Samantha realized how different they were, something she hadn't picked up on the first time around. Samantha had always wanted to have a smallish family, but Aidan wanted four kids. Samantha thought public school, with active participation from parents, was a great choice for a child's education, while Aidan really hoped his kids would be home-schooled. So before they could ever consider making a more lasting commitment, Samantha and Aidan had a *lot* to talk about. But at least they had these issues on their radar—a vast improvement from how things had worked in the past.

But for now, Samantha thought a vacation was exactly what she needed, considering she was going to be looking for a job when she got back to Minneapolis.

* * *

Heading down to the Riverfront . . .

When Gavin needed a moment to clear his head, he often walked a few miles down to the Riverfront, which offered a picturesque view of the mighty Mississippi from downtown Minneapolis. He loved watching the stillness of all that water. It was calming, even when he didn't necessarily feel calm himself.

After wrestling for weeks earlier in the summer with whether or not to continue to pursue his music career, Gavin felt like God was speaking to him more loudly every day. And the message was clear: The time had come to move on to a new vocation.

Gavin thought he'd feel more melancholy, doing what he was about to do, but instead he actually felt relieved to be letting go. Getting a record deal had consumed so many of his thoughts over the years. He'd daydreamed about how it would happen and how he'd feel once he signed on the dotted line. Like most musicians who wanted a shot at the big time, he'd wondered what it would be like to grace the cover of a magazine and what riveting, insightful comments he'd make in the accompanying interview.

Like many Christians pursuing the arts, Gavin also had hoped that somehow his songs would make a difference in people's lives.

Challenge them to pursue God. Encourage. Inspire. But as the days wore on, he found it increasingly more difficult to write about things that *mattered* in a pop song. Creatively, he was at an impasse; he needed to find another way to express what he had inside.

Gavin just couldn't do music anymore, and he had his recent marriage to thank for that. Sydney inspired him to want to do something more with his life. That's why he was going to start his seminary training during the spring semester.

As a symbolic reminder of his life's new direction, Gavin planned to walk down to the Riverfront to pray before he drove over to the Mentoring Club of Minneapolis to donate his beloved Martin. The Mentoring Club had started a program a few months back to give free music lessons to underprivileged kids. And Gavin was going to donate his guitar — and his time while he still lived in Minneapolis. Ever since he'd heard about the program, he thought it was pretty cool, but now ideas were converting to action, which thrilled him beyond belief. Gavin had other guitars, of course, but he felt it was important to get rid of the one he'd loved the most to symbolize his new direction. And surprisingly, he'd never felt better.

CHAPTER 12

A MODERN-DAY EMMA'S SECRET LIFE AS A SPY

There is a time for daring and a time for caution, and a wise man knows which is called for.

— JOHN KEATING (ROBIN WILLIAMS) IN *DEAD POETS SOCIETY*, 1989

IT SEEMED LIKE ANY OTHER ordinary Tuesday when I woke up. I made blueberry pancakes, then Gavin went to the studio to wrap up some final recording sessions with Jaguar. Afterward, he was getting together with his band to break the news that he was going back to school. Each of the guys already played in a few other groups, so Gavin was glad he wasn't going to put the guys in a bad spot financially. He would miss the company, though. He and his band had such a great time together on the road. Still, it wasn't like Gavin was dying. He was simply pursuing something else for a living. The guys could still get together to jam, hang out, play pool, or whatever they did in their free time. And I wouldn't have to worry about Gavin being on the road.

As for me, I had a to-do list a mile long. I was working on a couple of features for *Vogue* for Lucinda. I also had a few music and book reviews to finish up for other clients, along with this week's installment of "Lucy" and something I hadn't done in quite a while—a travel piece called "Five Great Dates in Chicago" for *Budget Travel*. Since I'd been there so many times over the years (and experienced some of my not-so-impressive dates there), it wasn't terribly difficult to write up. Because Chicago's such a fun city, narrowing down the date-night options proved to be a little challenging though. But it was a challenge I was up for—and excited about.

Getting settled into my cozy little home office, I noticed my cell phone (it's hard to miss actually, considering it's bright pink) on my desk and checked to see if I'd missed any calls. Turns out I'd missed not one but thirteen from Lucinda.

Why in the world had Lucinda called thirteen times? Weirder still, why hadn't she bothered to leave a message? She was always a mysterious one, that Lucinda.

I picked up my phone and dialed her number. "*Vogue*, this is Amber. How may I direct your call?"

Hmmm, Amber was new. Seems like they had a new receptionist every week at *Vogue*. "Lucinda Buffington, please," I said brightly.

"May I tell her who's calling?"

"Yes, it's Sydney Williams."

"Oh, Sydney, it looks like Lucinda is on the other line. Would you like to leave a voice message?"

"Sure," I said. Some of us still had the common sense to leave messages, after all.

Minutes after I dug in and started working on the Chicago piece, I got a text from Lucinda.

CALL ME. CODE RED.

Code red? What was this, a hospital? A matter of national

security? Um, I don't think so. And why didn't Lucinda just call me back rather than texting me? My time was important too. Didn't she understand that?

Like a good friend/diligent employee, I called her back immediately. "Finally," Lucinda said, not even saying hello.

"Well, hello to you too," I said with a laugh. "What's up? Has Jude Law announced that he's going to marry you in *Us Weekly*? Or is it something more tragic like your precious black card being denied at Barneys?"

"Ha ha ha, always full of jokes, aren't you?" Lucinda said somberly. "Actually, I need your help with something. A mission."

"Uh-oh. The last time you needed my help with something, it involved setting you up with a guy named Elton," I replied. "What's making me have to get all Sydney Bristow for you?"

"If it were only that easy," Lucinda said. "The Elton incident was a piece of cake."

"Is it legal?" I asked. "You're not wanting me to hunt down some diet pills that aren't even approved by the FDA, are you?"

"I've never been slimmer," Lucinda said proudly. "I'm on the I-think-my-boyfriend-may-be-cheating-on-me diet, which consists of Red Bull and ice water. And that brings me to that favor."

"I don't think I like the sound of this," I said. "Don't you have an assistant to get you more Red Bull?"

"Of course I do. Just hear me out, Syd," Lucinda said in a voice that sounded desperate. "Philip is actually in Minneapolis as we speak, talking to investors about possibly opening a Pinkberry in the Twin Cities."

"That's cool," I said. "So what's the problem?"

"Well, I saw on his BlackBerry that a bunch of the investors are taking him to an exclusive Radiohead gig at the Fine Line tonight as a thank-you for coming to town," Lucinda said.

"What's wrong with seeing Radiohead?" I asked bluntly. "I'm still failing to see what's wrong with this picture."

Trying her best to explain, Lucinda said, "Whenever Philip and I have talked lately, something just hasn't felt right. He's been uncharacteristically preoccupied. Not as affectionate in his tone," Lucinda said. "And the woman who set up the meeting was always really flirty whenever she called Philip. They'd talk way too long, laugh constantly." She paused and lowered her voice. "I'm concerned that maybe there's something going on there."

"Lucinda, I am so sorry," I said. "What exactly do you want me to do? Wait—I'm sure you've got a plan all worked out." She missed the irony.

"Very perceptive," Lucinda said. "Basically, I'd like you to go to the show and see if there's any funny business going on."

"What?" I said. "You want me to *spy* on your boyfriend?"

"Is that a problem?" Lucinda said.

I had to take another tack. "I've been hearing about that show, and apparently it's a closed event," I said. "I'm not on the guest list."

"You know everyone in the music biz up there; you can get on the list," Lucinda said. "Shouldn't be too difficult—everybody likes you."

"Flattery will get you nowhere," I said. "Even if I got in, I'm not so sure I want to be spying on Philip. What if he sees me and wonders why I'm there?"

"C'mon, Sydney, you're resourceful," Lucinda whined. "Make something up. A little white lie."

She's begging! It hit me: She must really, really like Philip to make herself so vulnerable. I didn't know what to do.

"Lucinda, I can't spy on your boyfriend." There. I'd said it. "I just don't feel comfortable doing that." How could she possibly refute that?

"Well, I see your mind is made up," Lucinda said. "No more assignments for *Vogue* then!"

"What?" She had to be joking. "Lucinda . . . I did a feature on Yanni for you, for heaven's sake!"

That calmed her down. "I'm sorry, that was out of line." She paused. "But this thing with Philip is driving me crazy."

I could tell.

Taking a much softer tone, Lucinda opened up. "This has been the best three months of my life, and I'm so afraid—" She stopped, and I could hear her sigh. "I'm so afraid he'll get bored with me and go after some new hot thang," she confessed. "Do you think Philip would do that?"

"I don't know," I began. "But if he's put up with you for this long, I'd say he's a keeper."

"Very funny, Syd."

"Have you tried talking to him?" I asked. "Does he have a wandering eye? Have you seen him checking out other women?"

"No," Lucinda said. "But I would feel better if you were at that concert. What if I get in touch with Radiohead's people and get you the comps? All you'd have to do is show up. If you *happened* to see Philip, then . . ."

"Okay, okay," I said. "I'll go to the concert. But no guarantees about Philip."

"That's good enough for me," Lucinda said. "I'll text you when you're confirmed for the guest list."

Sigh. Why did I let Lucinda talk me into this? I mean, I adore

Radiohead; who doesn't? But are the free tickets really worth this much trouble? My guess is that Emma didn't have to put up with shenanigans like this.

* * *

A new home sweet home for Eli . . .

After three months, Eli finally had the majority of his stuff unpacked at his brand-new digs just outside of Boston. Once Eli walked the line at graduation, he'd made a very important decision about his life: He needed to move.

He couldn't bear seeing Samantha's face or the places that made him think of her any longer. Hearing her name called out at the ceremony and seeing Aidan there cheering her on made him sick to his stomach. Seriously, he wanted to vomit. He held it together because his family was in the audience. They'd been so supportive and encouraging—to the point of being annoying sometimes. But at least Eli knew they cared.

So he knew he had to get out of the Twin Cities. But where would he move? He turned on the travel channel once he got home. Spain—that was definitely out of the question. Too expensive. Too far away. And his mom just might murder him. Not Spain, then. He had a few friends in Denver. Yeah, Denver sounded good. Skiing, the Rocky Mountains, sipping cocoa by the chalet with cute girls dressed in pink winter coats and scarves.

Then Eli remembered he couldn't move there either: He and Sam had gone skiing there last winter.

Tired, frustrated, and getting grumpier by the moment, Eli flipped on the radio, and a simple, inane pop song by Augustana called "Boston" gave him an idea.

A new life. That's exactly what Eli wanted. He'd never heard of the band that sang the song until the deejay said its name—Augustana. But now Eli might possibly be the group's biggest fan. Boston sounded like the perfect place to start over, even if he had only visited once on a class field trip back in high school. So while he continued to pursue leads in the Twin Cities, he started exploring the Boston job market (thank goodness for the Internet) as well.

And lo and behold, there were so many more interesting opportunities there. He applied to be an entry-level financial analyst. After a couple of weeks of working at Gap and following up on leads, Eli had a few promising phone interviews that could lead to a great career once he relocated. So he did.

Eli had given his two weeks' notice back in early June. Then he packed his car (he didn't have much) and made the nearly twenty-three-hour trek east. He couldn't really afford to live in Boston proper, so he found a great place in North Cambridge that fit his budget for now.

The adjustment had been going really well. He got hired as an entry-level accountant at Century Bank. And he was getting his bearings around Beantown too. When Eli wasn't working (which sure beat going to school by a long shot), he was busy getting acquainted with his new city. He loved how the Bostonians seemed to have an appreciation for history. There weren't as many new houses, and the neighborhoods were fun to explore, especially around the Harvard campus.

He kept in touch with a couple of friends back in Minnesota, but he'd deliberately made it a point to focus on his new life rather than dwell on the past. He'd been exploring a new church service each week and even checked into auditing a couple of weekend literature classes at Boston College—just because he could.

Some days were more difficult than others, but Eli was slowly starting to get over Samantha. Forgiving her was the easy part—forgetting wasn't quite as simple. But with each passing day, he knew he was going in the right direction. And for now, that was just fine with him.

＊　＊　＊

A working coffee break in downtown Minneapolis . . .

After getting my private-investigation assignment from Lucinda earlier today, it hadn't been easy to concentrate on work. But I did manage to finish my travel piece on Chicago and was now in the middle of selecting my second letter for this week's "Lucy for the Lovelorn" column. But for some reason I couldn't bear being at my home office for even five more minutes, so I relocated to a nearby Starbucks, where I could sip a Caramel Macchiato and type away on my MacBook at the same time—not a bad way to spend an afternoon, if I do say so myself.

I selected the following letter for "Lucy" because I could relate to it so well when I was single. It's funny how competitive/jealous your girlfriends can be when you're dating (and they're not).

> *Dear Lucy,*
> *I started seeing this great guy named Max a couple*
> *of weeks ago. I know it's probably still too early to*
> *see his flaws, but so far, he's been everything I've*
> *ever wanted. He's kind, funny, cute, adventurous,*
> *and likes to ride motorcycles like I do.*

But like most guys, Max has a past. His wife left him about six months ago when she fell out of love with him and fell in love with someone else. Definitely a sad situation, but he's worked through it.

Now that I'm so happy, my girlfriends call me "the rebound girl." They say his "shady" past means we won't have much of a future. I know they don't sound like good friends, but seriously these are some of my closest girls. What can I do to convince them Max is a great guy?

Sincerely,
Amelia

Darling Amelia,
What I'd love to get you is a new group of girlfriends. But since you say they're the real deal, I'll have to take your word for it. In the meantime, forget 'em and have fun with Max. Get to know him and make sure he's still everything you want in a guy, because it sounds like no matter what you do, these girls will be pea green with jealousy as long as you have a man and they don't. So don't waste your precious time worrying about what these girls think about your guy's past. Believe it or not, they have one too.

Hope that helps!
Love,
Lucy

After I submitted my latest "Lucy" column and downed every last drop of coffee, I decided to head back home and take a quick nap before I hit that Radiohead concert.

❋ ❋ ❋

After filling Gavin in on tonight's covert operation at the Fine Line, he warned me that he wouldn't be participating in my spying antics. Then he reassured me that if I ended up going to the slammer, he would come and visit me every week and bring me peanut M&M'S and *Us Weekly*. Hey, what are husbands for but to bring you treats while you don the orange jumpsuit? Guess that means I could save my one phone call for Jane (if she were talking to me) or Sam (if I could ever get in touch with her since Aidan has started monopolizing her time) or my mom (if she ever learned how to use the call waiting feature on her cell phone).

I planned to be subtle, though, so I was sure jail wasn't in the cards for me. Thank goodness — orange isn't exactly my color.

I was still a bit sleepy since I'd only napped for fifteen minutes. Just as I was on the verge of dreamland — twice — Lucinda called to make sure everything was set. She was extremely thorough when she wanted to be. So to help me wake up, Gavin and I stopped off at Moose & Sadie's for a quick cup of java before we headed over to the Fine Line.

Just a few blocks from our condo, the Fine Line is one of my favorite venues in downtown Minneapolis. Nestled inside a historic building, it's the perfect size (in my humble, music critic opinion) for a terrific show. It's not too big and not too small, and seeing Radiohead there would be a once-in-a-lifetime occurrence, the way seeing Halley's Comet was for stargazers. Radiohead rarely tours the States, so when they come around, you have to buy tickets the second they go on sale or they're gone. Unfortunately, I'm speaking from experience here, as it's happened to me not once but twice.

Now, thanks to press privileges, I was finally going to see one of the bands I'd yet to see play. I couldn't wait (nor could Gavin) to hear front man Thom Yorke sing his falsetto-lovin' heart out.

After Gavin and I got situated inside, I scanned the room for anyone who looked like Philip.

"See him?" Gavin asked curiously as I gave the room the once-over. And then the twice-over. Not yet.

"It's still a little early." I sighed. "Maybe he'll cruise in after the opening act."

"Sure," Gavin said. He still thought I was nuts to be doing this. "Remember when I played here just before we got engaged?"

"I do," I said with a grin. "I was a very proud girlfriend. You sounded absolutely incredible."

"Uh, you're a little biased, since I swept you off your feet and all," Gavin said, and he squeezed my hand.

Giving his hand a little squeeze back, I said, "Nope. Not biased in the least. You are a very talented singer-songwriter."

"Don't you mean *were*?" Gavin said.

"Just because you're moving on doesn't make you any less talented," I said reassuringly. "You're just flexing a different muscle with this seminary adventure. You're multitalented."

"Well, that's good," Gavin said. "Because I gave my Martin away yesterday."

"You *what?*" I asked.

"Yep, someone else will be the proud owner," Gavin said. "A new chapter of my life is officially unfolding."

CHAPTER 13

I'M NOT SURE HOW MATT DAMON DOES IT . . .

Stories don't always end where their authors intended. But
there is joy in following them, wherever they take us.

—BEATRIX POTTER (RENÉE ZELLWEGER) IN *MISS POTTER*, 2006

I'M PRETTY SURE EMMA never pursued a career in espionage,
and I'm not planning to either. The spy life is clearly not the
life for me. I was sweating, and nothing had even happened yet.
Maybe I would've felt better if I was incognito. Some Jackie O.
shades, a stylish trench like Emma Peel, and I'd be set.

Okay, Gavin said that wouldn't even help.

So there I was, the novice spy, trying to keep my eyes peeled
for Philip. Wait! Was that him?

I walked over to the other side of the room to get a better look.
Yep, that had to be him. With all the boldness I could muster, I
tapped him on the shoulder as Gavin watched from across the
room. I had no idea what I was going to say next, so I started with
his name.

"Philip?"

"Sorry, love, you must have had too much to drink," he said
in a British accent. Guess he must have been one of the roadies.

Can we say *embarrassing*? Come to think of it, up close that guy really didn't look much like Philip at all. My frazzled nerves must have been distorting my vision.

Then out of the corner of my eye, I spotted him. Yes, without a doubt, that was the guy I met at the bagel shop in Manhattan. And he was with an attractive brunette who was hanging all over him. Not very professional, to say the least.

Philip seemed pretty friendly with her too. Well, actually, no: Now that I got a longer look, he was being polite. That brunette looked like she might be drunk. Still, I knew this wasn't good news. Keeping my eyes on them for a few minutes, I picked up on some flirty vibes, but really nothing criminal.

Deciding my mission was officially accomplished, I walked back over to where Gavin was standing, and we enjoyed the concert.

In a strictly musical sense, Radiohead was even better than I'd expected. Not only did the band sound much better live than on disc (never an easy feat), the set list was surprisingly diverse. Lead singer Thom Yorke is known for being a bit persnickety—even difficult—when it comes to choosing the set list. He usually favors the recent album, while the fans desperately want to hear hits like "Creep," "Karma Police," and "Fake Plastic Trees." But Radiohead surprised us: They played a wealth of songs from their latest project and an acoustic set of popular songs too.

It was a great show. But I was worried about disappointing Lucinda.

I held off calling her as long as humanly possible. But then around eleven, I bit the bullet and called her. Even though it was midnight her time, I figured she'd still be awake, eagerly awaiting my news.

"Hello?" she said calmly. "So what's the verdict?"

Wow, she wasted no time at all.

I carefully selected my words. "I did see Philip at the show," I said.

"And? C'mon, Syd, you can't leave me hanging. Was he with her?"

"He was talking to some girl," I said nervously. "But—"

"I knew it!" she said. "Philip's cheating on me!"

As rationally and calmly as possible, I tried to reassure her. "You don't know that for sure. He's there on business. Maybe he was just being nice in a professional way. That's what it looked like."

"Whatever," Lucinda said. "Thanks for checking. I best get my beauty sleep. I don't want to look like an old hag the next time I see him."

Lucinda sure is dramatic, isn't she?

After I vented to Gavin a little (he's got this way of calming me down post-Lucinda), we went to sleep with visions of Radiohead dancing in our heads.

* * *

More than 1,500 miles away at LAX . . .

It was just after nine a.m. LA time, and Jane was making her way to baggage claim. Aside from her family, Jane hadn't told anyone she was in La La Land. She wasn't trying to be mysterious, but she didn't want to tell too many people about her job interview at a news station in Los Angeles because she wasn't positive she'd get the position. Jane also knew she was a smidge underqualified, but her boss at KARE-11 had encouraged her to give it a shot. Like many local news anchors, Jane hoped to move up the ranks, and she knew she'd have to leave Minneapolis to do that.

And you couldn't get much better than Los Angeles. The LA peeps really liked her audition tape and had offered to fly her out for a face-to-face, so that was a promising sign, right?

After picking up her luggage, she hailed a cab and made her way to her hotel, the Best Western Carlyle Inn, which wasn't far from Rodeo Drive in Beverly Hills on the paparazzi-friendly haven of Robertson Boulevard.

While Jane loved Los Angeles (she'd grown up there, after all), the seemingly never-ending parking lot of traffic was a sobering reminder of what her daily commute would be like if she relocated. But she knew that working at the LA station would have its perks too — prestige, a greater variety of stories to report on, an opportunity to live closer to family. Celebrities too. It could be exciting and fulfilling.

As Jane continued her journey to Bev Hills in the slow-moving taxi, she felt a tug on her heart to tell one person what she was up to: Sydney. She was still annoyed about the Campbell situation, but it wasn't really Sydney's fault. Jane knew that deep down. The problem was that Jane had felt something she hadn't felt in a long time: hope. And hope, especially hope for a lasting relationship, was a tricky thing. She'd been comfortable (or at least that's what she told herself) about being cold and cynical toward the opposite sex. It was just easier that way when guys seemed to ask everyone out but her. Or mentioned that she was "intimidating." Sydney had been the one who encouraged her to get out of her comfort zone and try again.

So she had poured a lot of energy and feelings into Campbell.

And when Campbell seemed to prove again and again that he only had friendship on his mind, Jane couldn't help getting frustrated. She began to wonder what was wrong with her. Jane felt rejected all over again and held her friend, her dear friend, responsible. As she reached for her cell phone to call her, Jane already started to feel better. She hoped Sydney was around for a chat.

Ringing. Ringing. Ringing. *Please no voice mail,* Jane thought. *I don't want to leave a message.*

"Hello?"

"Sydney, it's Jane."

✻ ✻ ✻

Nashville comes calling Gavin . . .

Whether it was in regard to meeting his wife or landing a few of his early songwriting gigs, Gavin knew that God's timing was seldom the same as his. He always summed it up by saying, "Abba's wristwatch has a tick-tock all its own."

On the other hand, just because Gavin knew this about God's timing didn't mean his life was any easier. Like most people, he liked to know precisely what the next phase of his life was going to look like. And now that he was happily married, he also wanted Sydney to be taken care of. Of course, Gavin knew that God would always provide, but as the man of the house, he had a healthy dose of male pride and wanted all the details in place. He had already gotten the ball rolling by applying to Vanderbilt Divinity School in Nashville, Trinity Evangelical Divinity School in Chicago, and Bethel Seminary in St. Paul, but he didn't know where he and Sydney would end up.

As Gavin was thinking about this and praying about God's continued peace in an uncertain time of his life, his phone rang. *A 615 area code—that's Nashville. Maybe it's a Vanderbilt rep letting me know they received my application.*

"Is this Gavin Williams?" an unfamiliar male voice asked.

"Speaking," Gavin said.

"This is George Evans from Lonely Hearts Publishing," he said. "How's it going?"

"Doing well," Gavin said, wondering what this could be about.

"Listen, Gavin, we've been hearing some great songs around town, and every time we ask about the songwriter, your name comes up. And Jaguar Jones played 'Talk to Me' for us a couple of days ago. So we were wondering if you might consider an exploratory meeting with us about signing a publishing deal."

"Wow. That's—wow, I can't believe this," Gavin said.

"We really liked your song. It's catchy," George said. "Will you think it over and let us know?"

"That's the best compliment I've ever received," Gavin said. "Thank you so much. I won't keep you hangin' for long."

"I'll look forward to hearing from you soon, then," George said. "You've got my number? Call me day or night."

Gavin stared at his phone and shook his head. If someone had told him he'd be offered a shot at a publishing deal right after he gave his favorite guitar to charity, he never would've believed it. That was so like God. He knew his resolve was being tested, but before he called George back to decline his kind offer, he had to tell Sydney.

* * *

It's deadline time again . . .

You know how Joni Mitchell says that someone doesn't know what they've got till it's gone? I never realized how much I appreciated Jane's friendship until it was on hiatus. She's a great girl with insecurities just like the rest of us. It's always difficult for me to remember that because Jane is near perfect in my book. But after she explained where she was coming from, it all started to make sense. I knew she had rejection issues, but I guess I just never knew how serious they were. Silly Campbell. Why didn't he ask her out? Maybe I could get to the bottom of that.

In the meantime, I had to get to the bottom of some deadlines. Wait. Was that Gavin calling? Okay, I'd take this call first, then the deadlines.

❋ ❋ ❋

Twenty minutes and a whole lot of shock later . . .

Nashville. What was it about that place? I couldn't seem to get away from it. At least in terms of the men who've been in my life. After years of wondering if it would ever happen, Gavin had been offered a shot at a publishing deal. And since he knew he wasn't supposed to accept what would've been the opportunity of a lifetime because it wasn't the right direction for his life right now, the timing was even more curious.

Due to my own curiosity about the terms of the deal, I wanted to tell Gavin to accept the meeting. But he felt it would be a waste of time, and rightly so. It wasn't the writer's block that had gotten him down but the feeling that he could be doing something more meaningful with his life. His motivation for doing music wasn't always the right one, and he was tired of trying to justify his career choice. It wasn't that music was bad or didn't have potential as a meaningful career; it was just time to move on. If Gavin and I did end up in Nashville, it'd be for an entirely different purpose, something both he and I were okay with.

* * *

So far so good for Jane . . .

As Jane walked down the hallway of the tastefully decorated office, she didn't feel quite as nervous as she thought she might. You can say that clothes don't make the man, but a woman will tell you otherwise. Jane had paid a fortune for the immaculately tailored Burberry suit she was wearing, and she knew it looked great. And she felt great too. It made her feel strong and classy and confident. Now Jane hoped that Mr. Frank Hawkins and his staff would also be a fan of the suit—and of her.

CHAPTER 14

CALIFORNIA: FRIEND OR FOE?

I was still waiting for everything to start, and now it's over.
—HOLLIE BAYLOR (SUSAN SARANDON) IN *ELIZABETHTOWN*, 2005

THE NEXT COUPLE OF days passed quickly, and before Samantha knew it, Friday (aka Destination: San Francisco) had finally arrived. She was usually a last-minute packer, but she was so fired up about leaving town with Aidan that she'd been ready to go for days. What a dork! But she couldn't help herself. It wasn't every day that a girl got to take a romantic vacation with her significant other.

She had packed a variety of clothes for a variety of occasions. Sweaters for those chilly evenings strolling around Golden Gate Park. Flirty dresses for romantic nights on the town. Sneakers and cute gym shorts for when they went running. Like a good Girl Scout, she was prepared.

Even though Sydney didn't exactly approve of Samantha and Aidan's little getaway—she thought it was much too early for them to be vacationing together, given their rocky history—always the reliable sister, she was giving Sam a ride to the airport. In fact, if Friday afternoon traffic wasn't too much of a bear, Sydney would be at Samantha's place in about twenty minutes, giving them

175

plenty of time to get to the airport so Sam and Aidan could make the seven thirty p.m. flight.

Aidan was stuck at the Wells Fargo office until four o'clock, so he was going to have to drive separately. For some reason, he had seemed a little tense to Samantha all week long. Maybe it was because he was going to have to make a decision about whether to go back to India soon. Or perhaps it was because his boss had been out of town all week, leaving Aidan to pick up the slack. But whatever it was, Samantha hoped that San Francisco would provide a welcome respite—because like the Incredible Hulk, Aidan wasn't much fun to be around when he was angry. Or tense, for that matter.

❊ ❊ ❊

Yea or nay? Jane wants to know . . .

After a long day of traveling from Los Angeles back to Minneapolis yesterday, Jane was exhausted but keyed up at the same time. The mix of not enough sleep and nervous anticipation wasn't a good one as she wondered when the people at KCAL planned to call. Sure, they'd said sometime Friday, but it was already late afternoon, and Jane began to wonder if they'd forgotten about her. Maybe her power suit hadn't been as powerful as she'd hoped. Maybe they'd gone with someone prettier, thinner, more qualified. This was Los Angeles, after all. The same rules probably didn't apply for who would work on air and who wouldn't.

Then Jane remembered the time difference. They were two hours behind, which was going to make it all the more frustrating because their window of time had just extended by two hours.

She drummed her fingertips nervously on her dining room table, then sighed.

She had to do something to pass the time or she'd go crazy. So Jane popped in one of her favorite movies, *Broadcast News*. It was a bit dated (1987, to be exact) and overly dramatic, but she loved Holly Hunter's performance as the dedicated newswoman who was not only equal with her male counterparts but maybe even sharper. The movie had been made way before female empowerment was cool in television shows and movies too. Then, as the movie's story unfolded, Jane had what she thought was a pretty significant epiphany about Campbell.

Perhaps it's my ambitions that have scared Campbell off, she thought. *Maybe Campbell's more into the silent, submissive type who just agrees with whatever he says. Maybe I should just be single, like the woman in* Broadcast News. *She's happy with her work, her life. She doesn't need men to make her happy . . .*

Then, right in the middle of her mental tirade, Jane's phone rang. It was Campbell. *Okay, forget all of that . . . I still want him to like me.*

"Hey, Jane," Campbell said. "How's it going?" Jane even liked the way Campbell said her name in that cute, slightly Southern accent of his. How pathetic was that?

"I'm a little stressed at the moment actually," she responded, slightly surprised that she hadn't offered up a more generic reply.

"What's making you so stressed?"

"Well . . ." She wondered if she should tell him. "I'm actually waiting on a pretty important call," she said. "I just interviewed for a job at a station in LA."

"Los Angeles, huh?" Campbell said. He sounded slightly disappointed—a positive development. "I guess that explains why you haven't been at group lately."

"Nah, it has nothing to do with that," Jane said. "I just needed a break."

"We've really missed you," Campbell said softly. "I know I'm being presumptuous, but may I ask why?"

"You could, but I'm not sure I'd give you a straight answer," Jane offered.

"That's honest," Campbell said with a laugh. "But what if I really, really wanted to know?"

"You *really* want to know?" Jane asked.

"I do," Campbell said. "You know, if you don't mind and all."

"Um, well, hmmm—"

"You know what? That explains everything," Campbell said, laughing even harder now. "Glad we got that all cleared up."

Then, choosing her words carefully, Jane said, "Honestly, the reason I haven't been coming to group is because I'm a little frustrated with you."

"Frustrated with me?" Campbell asked curiously. "What about?"

"I don't know how to put it," Jane said. "I wasn't ever expecting to have to talk about it."

"Whatever it is, Jane, you can say it to me," Campbell said. "Whether it's now, two weeks from now, two years from now . . . but I hope it's not two years from now because you've got me all curious—"

"Here's the deal," Jane began. "Ever since Sydney's luau a while ago, I thought—gosh, this is so hard."

"What did you think?"

"I thought you might have feelings for me," Jane said. "And

with all our flirting and hanging out, I guess I thought it might lead somewhere, so I was frustrated when nothing materialized, and I didn't want to see you for a while. There, I've said it."

Campbell didn't say anything for a few seconds, and the silence was almost unbearable for Jane. It was like a jury deliberating a verdict in complete silence. It was eerie and unnerving, and she didn't like it one bit. What was he thinking, and why did she suddenly feel sick to her stomach?

Then, breaking the silence, Campbell spoke. "Boy, I so didn't see that coming," he began. "I'm a little stunned, to be perfectly frank."

Jane anticipated the worst. She already didn't like where this was headed and wished Campbell would hurry up and say it—rip off the Band-Aid with one quick motion rather than torture her with a long, drawn-out explanation.

"I honestly had no idea that you had feelings for me in that way. I'm honored, actually, because I think you're quite beautiful," Campbell said. "But—"

Oh no, here it comes, Jane thought. *Here comes the "you're a great girl, but—" speech.*

"As the singles' pastor, I don't know that I'm comfortable having a relationship with someone in the group," Campbell said. "I don't know if it's fair to everyone else."

"But I haven't been coming to the group," Jane pointed out. "Remember I've been on hiatus?"

"Technically, you're right," Campbell said with a laugh. "But everyone in the group knows you, and it could make them feel uncomfortable to know that their singles' pastor is dating a congregant."

"A congregant? A congregant? That's all I am to you?" Jane

said, her voice getting louder by the second. "So if I'd never come to group, you would've considered dating me?"

"Please don't be angry," Campbell said. "Remember, I didn't know you felt this way. I'm not the guy girls typically go for. I'm like the big brother, never the love interest. I don't know *how* to be the love interest."

"That really surprises me."

"What?"

"The whole big brother thing," Jane replied. "You're a stud and apparently you don't even know it. That's very cute."

"I don't know about *that*," Campbell said. "I haven't had a good track record with dating."

"That makes two of us," Jane said. "Apparently I can't even read the signals right."

"Don't beat yourself up," Campbell said. "You're gorgeous. You're going to have no trouble at all finding a guy. Maybe LA is the ticket."

"Yeah, the land of supermodels," Jane said sarcastically. "My dating life is *so* not going to improve if I move there."

"You never know," Campbell said. "Supermodels probably get pretty old after a while."

"Sure — outer beauty is such a curse," Jane said with a laugh, then added, "I'm glad I got this off my chest, Campbell. Even if I didn't get the desired result."

"That's good to hear," Campbell said. "I apologize for sending mixed signals. I didn't mean to."

"Apology accepted. I'm sure I was just reading too much into things," Jane said. "You know, it was Sydney who suggested we'd make a great couple. That luau was for us."

"Really? Wow," Campbell said in his best aw-shucks tone. "It was a great party. Great food. Great ambience. A lot of fun."

"Thanks," Jane said. "Sydney likes playing matchmaker, and now she's struck out twice for me."

"The other was the feet guy, right?" Campbell said.

"I can't believe you remember that."

"A story like that is pretty unforgettable," Campbell said. "But can I just say one thing?"

"Sure," Jane said. "Anything."

"I don't think you really need a matchmaker," Campbell said. "I'm sure you've heard this a million times, so forgive me if I sound like a broken record. But the best things come when we aren't expecting them. Maybe you're trying a little too hard to make a relationship happen. It's best when they happen naturally."

Jane thought about that for a second. *Campbell is probably right, but I so hate hearing that right now.*

"Yeah, I've heard that," Jane said. "But the waiting part isn't easy."

"No kidding," Campbell said. "Try being a thirty-year-old virgin."

Jane laughed, her face turning a little red. "Now, Campbell, that's TMI."

"Sorry," he said.

"No need to apologize. It may be TMI, but . . . I wish I could say the same," Jane said.

After another awkward silence, Campbell filled the conversation gap.

"Okay, now I'm the one who wishes he hadn't brought that up, so . . . lemme just ask this—"

"Yeah?"

"Would you consider coming back to group sometime?"

Campbell asked. "I think everyone would really like that."

"I'll think about it," Jane said.

"All right. That's a good start. I'll take that," Campbell said.

＊　＊　＊

San Francisco, here we are . . .

It took Aidan the duration of the flight to get calm, and Samantha made sure to give him his space. Whatever was wrong with him, she didn't want it to spoil their trip, so she didn't ask. He didn't exactly look in the mood to chat with that scowl on his face.

After landing in San Francisco and picking up their baggage, Aidan finally spoke up. "Thanks for being patient with me on the flight. It was a long day at work."

"I guessed something like that," Samantha said. "But now that we're on vacation, there won't be a care in the world."

"I don't know about *that*," he said. "But I bet I'll feel better about everything. Especially because I'm here with you." Then he leaned over and kissed Samantha's cheek, and she returned the gesture on his lips.

"Mmmm," he said. "I think your kiss just helped me get out of my funk."

"Always glad to be of assistance."

As they made their way to the rental car, the cool, crisp air revived the wave of sleepiness that had plagued them on the plane. Here they were in this gorgeous city and were definitely in need of sustenance. So before they even checked in at the hotel, they decided that finding a dinner spot was their first priority.

＊　＊　＊

Jane is one popular girl today . . .

Not long after Jane got off the phone with Campbell (quite the revealing conversation, that's for sure), her phone rang again. And the area code was 310—definitely Los Angeles. She took a deep breath and answered.

"Is this Jane?" The woman used a professional tone.

"Yes, it is."

"This is Amanda with KCAL," she said. "I have good news and bad news for you."

Jane gulped. "Okay. I didn't get the job."

"Unfortunately, there was someone more qualified for that particular position," Amanda said. "But the good news is that we'd still like to offer you a job as our lead news writer. We think you've got a great nose for news; your clips were outstanding—"

"Thanks," Jane said. "I really appreciate that."

"I know it's not the job you want," Amanda said. "But it could be a stepping-stone to the position you want here. So think it over and let us know."

"I will," Jane said. "Thank you so much for the opportunity."

"No problem," Amanda said. "I can give you until Monday for an answer."

"Sure thing," Jane said. "I'll let you know ASAP."

Mere seconds after Jane hung up the phone, she'd already begun analyzing the situation. It wasn't the position she really wanted, but it was an intriguing offer all the same. Would she want to move to Los Angeles to write news full-time? It definitely gave her food for thought and lots to pray about.

❋ ❋ ❋

Sharing seafood and talking about the future . . .

Samantha had never been to San Francisco before, but she figured seafood was sort of a no-brainer. So after asking a couple of random locals for recommendations on the best seafood place in town, they decided to see if there were any tables available for two hungry tourists in Union Square. Like you might expect for chic restaurants on a Friday night, though, the wait was in the neighborhood of two hours at most places.

"I might die of malnutrition by then," Samantha said. "Wanna grab something quick instead?"

"That works for me," Aidan said.

Spotting a Ghirardelli emporium nearby, they decided to eat their dinner in reverse—dessert first. "I don't know why, but I feel a bit naughty doing this, like I'm going to get grounded or something," Samantha said. "I can still hear my mom's voice in the back of my head: 'Sam, you can only have chocolate if you eat all your vegetables first.'"

"It's a good thing you're not living at home anymore, then, isn't it?" Aidan said mischievously. "So what kind are we thinking?"

"Milk chocolate and caramel. Dark chocolate and mint. Dark chocolate and raspberry. Those all sound delicious," Sam said. "How shall we choose?"

"One of each," Aidan said decisively. "I think that's the only option."

After Aidan paid for the treats, he opened the wrapper to the dark chocolate and raspberry and fed Sam a bite.

"I think I'd be game to eat dessert first from now on," Sam said, savoring the taste of chocolate. "But only if I'm with you."

CHAPTER 15

CABLE CARS, COLD FEET, AND OTHER
COMPLICATIONS

Try to be wrong once in a while. It'd do my ego good.

—NELSON MOSS (KEANU REEVES) IN *SWEET NOVEMBER*, 2001

B Y THE TIME SAM and Aidan got around to eating dinner
on Friday night, the best option ended up being Taco Bell.
They'd spent so much time walking around, talking, and enjoying the sights in Union Square that food was no longer a priority. All that Ghirardelli chocolate had taken the edge off their
hunger for quite a while.

The night ended abruptly around midnight when Sam
realized she just couldn't take another step. Given the time
change, of course, it felt much, much later than midnight.

It took Aidan roughly fifteen minutes to locate their hotel,
even driving speedily. After checking in and getting the bags all
situated, Samantha gave him a kiss good night, and they headed
to their respective rooms.

"Sure you're going to be all right, sweetie?" Aidan asked
with the gentle, reassuring concern of a parent caring for a sick
child.

"I'll manage," Sam said. "I think I need sleep more than anything."

"Okay. Good night," Aidan said. "I love you."

Did Aidan just say "I love you"? Samantha wondered. Maybe she was hearing things because she wasn't feeling well.

"What did you just say?" she said.

"I'm pretty sure I said, 'I love you,'" Aidan replied.

* * *

On the east coast, life is equally confusing . . .

Wild and crazy Friday nights were nothing out of the ordinary for Lucinda. But this one definitely broke protocol. She hadn't gone dancing at Bungalow 8 for ages. Since she'd started dating Philip, her life seemed to be straight off the pages of a fairy tale. Well, except that night when she thought he was cheating, of course, but that was just her insecurity talking. One long talk over the phone had pretty much settled all of that.

And after that misunderstanding, Philip really stepped it up in the showing-he-cared department. He bought Lucinda little gifts for no reason and showered her with flowers. He didn't care that she worked around the clock. He took her to dinner no matter how late it was. He wasn't needy, neglectful, annoying, or overbearing. Philip even took her to church on a regular basis, an entirely new experience for Lucinda, since her Sundays used to be spent sleeping in, shopping, and making her to-do list for the upcoming week.

Yet somehow, even though Lucinda couldn't ask for a better boyfriend, she felt like she'd lost a part of herself lately. Life seemed too good to be true with Philip, and she wasn't positive how she felt about that. She was used to chaos and being cheated on. Constant fighting. Guys who forgot her birthday or other significant events in her life. Somehow she didn't think she was capable of anything better. But Philip seemed like he had 'til-death-do-us-part potential.

When *Vogue* decided to host an elaborate schmooze-fest at Bungalow 8 to promote its latest issue, Lucinda didn't have a choice but to attend. And Philip had a meeting he couldn't get out of, so she was stuck attending alone.

It had been a long time since she'd gone anywhere without Philip, and Lucinda felt a little out of her element. So she immediately grabbed a martini and walked toward a few girls from work.

"Lucinda, is that you?" cooed Amanda Matthews, the resident beauty editor at *Vogue*. "I haven't seen you at one of these shindigs in ages."

"The party scene just hasn't been doing it for me lately," Lucinda said. "Too many late nights at work, I guess."

"Poor thing," Skye said. "Fortunately, there's lots of hotties here tonight to keep you good and distracted."

"Fortunately," Lucinda said, taking another sip of her drink.

"Oooh. I think I see some goodies over there," Amanda said as she walked toward a couple of guys standing by the appetizers. Still at loose ends, Lucinda followed.

She seemed to remember the guys from somewhere. But where? No matter how hard she tried, Lucinda couldn't recall where she'd seen them. Until one of them spoke to her.

"Correct me if I'm wrong, but have we met before?" the boyish-looking one said.

"You know, I was thinking the same thing," Lucinda said.

"But I seem to be drawing a blank. Refresh my memory, please."

"I'm Nick, and I'm actually in the current issue. I play in a band called Stillness," he said with a smile. "We did the interview with Sydney Williams, if that helps."

"Ah yes! I can't believe how silly I am," Lucinda said. Elton was standing beside Nick, and she snuck a glance at Elton's chiseled features. *I can't believe I forgot about him—he's still just fabulous.* "I'm Lucinda."

"We really enjoyed that interview with Sydney," Elton interjected. "She's a very knowledgeable music fan."

She was trying not to be too obvious about her admiration for Elton's toned physique, but it was hard. "Yeah, I think Sydney did a great job with that piece. She's one of my best writers."

Then Elton looked at his watch and said, "Lucinda, it was wonderful to see you again. I must dash. I have to pick up my girlfriend from the airport early tomorrow morning."

"Nice to see you." She was a little disappointed that Elton still had a girlfriend. Then, looking over at Nick, she said, "Want something from the bar? I was just about to get a refill."

"That would be great," Nick said, and he followed her to the bar.

"There's two empty seats here—wanna sit?" Lucinda asked.

"Sure," Nick said. "What are you drinking?"

"I'll have a dirty martini," she said.

Turning to the bartender, Nick said, "Dirty martini and a Diet Coke, please."

"Sure thing," the bartender said as he went to work on Lucinda's drink.

"So, Nick, Sydney told me that you're a nice guy. Is that true?"

"She told me you were nice too," he answered. "I was supposed to e-mail you—so we could get to know each other."

"We should do that," Lucinda said. "What do you like to do for fun?"

As Nick was about to answer, Lucinda impulsively kissed him—full on the lips. In the old days, Lucinda liked to kiss random strangers. It was quite the icebreaker. But this seemed to go horribly wrong.

Surprised by Lucinda's sudden advance, Nick pulled away before things got any crazier. "Um, I'm sorry," Nick said. "I may have been sending signals I didn't intend to. I think I'm going to call it a night. It was, uh, nice to meet you, Lucinda. Good night."

Strangely enough, the disgusted look on Nick's face was enough to jolt Lucinda back to reality. Kissing random strangers used to be such a rush. But with Philip in her life, she realized she didn't want to kiss anyone else, a pretty significant epiphany for someone like her.

Knowing what she knew now, Lucinda didn't want to stay at the party a second longer. And first thing tomorrow, Lucinda would tell Philip exactly what happened—even though the kiss with Nick was short-lived and meant nothing at all. Philip was unfailingly honest, and Lucinda had always fallen a little short in that department. But the time had come to turn over a new leaf.

✿　✿　✿

It's an eventful day in San Francisco . . .

When Samantha woke up on Saturday morning, it was nearly

eleven o'clock. The extra sleep had done her good because she didn't feel a trace of the funk she'd been feeling the night before.

Then she remembered those three little words that popped out of Aidan's mouth before they parted ways: "I love you." They would have to discuss that at some point today because they'd agreed from the beginning to take it slow.

Saying "I love you" felt like the fast track to Sam. But instead of freaking out and overanalyzing, a potent combination that had gotten her loads of heartache before, she tried to remain calm. After all, it might have been a mistake. They were both tired when it happened and in a new city on their first vacation together as a couple. Instead of normal food, they'd had Taco Bell for dinner. There were so many factors that came into play.

After showering and getting ready for the day, a ritual Samantha had whittled down to thirty minutes (a modern-day miracle, considering it used to be well over an hour), she gave Aidan a call on his cell.

"I wondered when you'd be waking up. Feeling any better?" Aidan said cheerfully. "I was starting to get worried that I was going to have to explore San Francisco all by myself."

"No such luck," Samantha joked. "I'm actually feeling a whole lot better. Must have been the sleep."

"Glad to hear it," Aidan said. "So if you're up to it, I was thinking we could go for a cable car ride and grab breakfast, lunch, whatever you're in the mood for."

"Sounds great," Samantha said. "How 'bout I meet you in the lobby in five minutes?"

"Perfect."

Exactly five minutes later, Aidan was waiting for Sam in the lobby. As she walked closer, he began to regret what he'd said last night. On the phone a few minutes ago, everything felt fine. But now? Not so much. Feeling nervous, slightly nauseated, and at a loss for words, Aidan leaned forward and gave her an awkward hug.

Finding Aidan's behavior a little bizarre, Samantha decided to ignore it for now. "So I'm looking forward to finally riding in a cable car. Ever since I saw my first Rice-A-Roni commercial, I just had to." *What kind of lame comment was that?* Samantha thought as soon as the words came out of her mouth. This was her boyfriend she was talking to. They needed to talk about this *I love you* business — and soon — because Aidan was acting a little funny too. His hug was totally limp, which was out of character.

"Yeah," Aidan said weakly. "That should be fun."

Once Aidan and Samantha reached the cable car stop, the crowd waiting was pretty large. Samantha immediately thought that if things didn't pick up soon, it just might be the longest few minutes of her life. After another minute of uncomfortable silence, she couldn't take it any longer. "Aidan, I think we need to talk," she said, just loud enough for his ears.

"Don't you want to wait until after the cable cars?" Aidan asked. "I mean, you've been wanting to do this for a while."

"I'm fairly confident the cable cars can wait," Samantha said. "We've got to sort some stuff out, Aidan."

They walked over to a bench nearby and sat down. After waiting a second to see if Aidan wanted to say something first, Samantha decided she'd better take the lead. "Are you freaking out because of what you said last night?" Samantha asked, surprised by how blunt that sounded.

"A little," Aidan said. "I thought I meant it at the moment. But in hindsight, it was a huge mistake."

"A huge mistake?" Samantha inquired. "I know we've only been together again for a little while, so it surprised me too. But calling it a huge mistake seems a bit dramatic, don't you think?"

"No," Aidan said. "We agreed to take it slow, and I goofed everything up."

"I don't think you goofed *everything* up."

"I just got caught up in the moment."

"And what moment would that be?" she said. "Saying good night?"

"I don't know, Samantha," Aidan said, sighing. "I think this whole trip may have been a mistake. Maybe it's just too soon for us to be vacationing together."

Samantha couldn't believe her ears. Was Aidan flaking out on her again?

"Well, we're already here. Shouldn't we make the best of it?" she asked. "We're just hanging out. But instead of the Twin Cities, we happen to be in this incredible city. Why not enjoy it?"

"I just don't know if I can—"

"You just don't know if you can do *what*, Aidan?" Samantha asked, getting more frustrated by the moment.

"I thought I was fine with everything. I was having a great time, and then I had to go and ruin everything by telling you I loved you—"

"And that's such a bad thing? It's not like we just met or something," she said, trying to be patient. "We have history."

"I know we do," Aidan began. "But what I think I want more than anything is to be back in India. I feel so much better serving than being served."

"But that's what's great about a relationship, Aidan," Samantha countered. "You get to do both."

"I guess I'm not ready for both," Aidan said.

Samantha wanted to bang her head against a wall. Kick something. Kick Aidan. Anything that would help her deal with the aggression she was feeling at this very moment. She'd put so much on the line for Aidan, and once again, he seemed to be hanging her out to dry.

"So what exactly are you saying?" Sam asked. "Do you want to break up?"

"Yeah, I think that's what I want, Sam," Aidan said calmly. "I think it's probably for the best."

"How can you say something like that so casually, so flippantly? Don't you care about me at all?" Sam just stared at him with her mouth open.

Aidan didn't know what to say. All he knew was that he needed to go back to Minneapolis—ASAP. "Sam, I know I don't deserve anything from you, but if you could give me a ride to the airport, that would be great."

Samantha couldn't believe what she was hearing. They hadn't even been here twenty-four hours, and he wanted to go home. *What is his problem?* Samantha thought as she debated how to respond without resorting to violence.

"You know what, today's your lucky day," Samantha said sarcastically. "There's no wait—we can leave immediately."

* * *

Kicking back is all that's on the agenda in Minneapolis . . .

After a long and eventful week, I was thrilled to finally have time to kick back and relax with Gavin. It had been way too long since my schedule didn't dictate the activities of the day.

And while my inner alarm clock woke me up a little earlier than I would've liked, it was nice to have the luxury of leisurely scanning the headlines of an actual newspaper rather than relying on the three-headline automated feed that appears on my customized Google page.

Once I finished with that, I thought I'd surprise Gavin with breakfast in bed. So as quietly as possible, I rustled up the ingredients to make Gavin an overstuffed omelet. Eggs are his favorite breakfast choice, and it didn't take long for the smell of butter and sautéed vegetables to waft through our condo, causing my cute, bleary-eyed husband to appear in the kitchen. "I knew I smelled something tasty cooking," Gavin said, surveying the contents of the skillet. "What's the special occasion?"

"Our much-deserved day off," I said.

"I'll eat to that," Gavin said. "Want me to make the toast?"

"I think I can handle it," I said. "You relax, and breakfast will be ready in a few."

Gavin didn't waste any time hangin' around the kitchen after hearing that. He went into the living room, flipped on the TV, and caught up on the sports highlights. Ah, the joys of a Saturday.

❋ ❋ ❋

Meanwhile, en route to SFO, Sam is still in shock . . .

Since Samantha was planning to hold on to the rental car and see the city with or without Aidan, she thought it would be far more convenient if she were the one driving to the airport.

They made the trip in complete silence, save for a few long, impatient sighs here and there, while Samantha occasionally wondered if she was stuck in the middle of a bad dream. Was she really taking Aidan to the airport? Right now, the whole situation felt about as real as Gwen Stefani's hair color.

In the passenger's seat, Aidan was comfortably numb. If he simply maintained his focus on the passing scenery, he'd be scot-free in a matter of minutes—no strings attached. As much as he wanted to believe he was capable of a functional relationship with a great girl like Sam, he'd quickly realized he still wasn't there. So it was far easier to be a jerk and end things horribly than to really address his fears, insecurities, and emotional baggage.

Sure, his mom would be disappointed to hear that the relationship had ended (again), but maybe that's exactly what she half-expected. A tiger can't really change his stripes, right? And if that's the case, can a chronic commitment-phobe change his ways? Maybe other guys could, but Aidan wasn't sure he was one of them. Even if he could take back what he had said to Sam in a moment of weakness, would it have made any difference in the end? Would he and Sam have run off into the sunset and lived happily ever after?

Now Aidan would never know. And maybe that was all right with him.

Pulling up to the Northwest terminal, Sam felt a few tears roll down her face. As much as she wanted to stay tough, her emotions got the best of her. In her favorite movies, the protagonist always had some brilliant speech in a moment like this—something witty that made the audience cheer once she was finished. But Samantha had no such speech—only a few choice words straight from her heart.

"I'm at a loss, Aidan," Samantha began. "I have no idea what to say to you except that I never want to talk to you again. So when you eventually realize that something went seriously wrong here — and I'm sure you will — I don't want you to e-mail. I don't want you to call. And whatever you do, don't show up somewhere you think I might be. Because even if I'm there, I won't be speaking with you, no matter what."

Aidan didn't bother responding. Really, what could he say that would make an ounce of difference? Samantha was justified in her rant, and he just wanted to get home.

Moments later, pulling his suitcase along with him, Aidan walked out of Samantha's sight for the last time, leaving not only Samantha in San Francisco, but part of his heart too. Unfortunately, he was way too proud to fully comprehend it yet.

CHAPTER 16

YES, THE TRUTH HURTS, SO SUE ME

Strange. But even when you know it has to end, when it
finally does, you always get that inevitable twinge: Have I
done the right thing?

—ALFIE (JUDE LAW) IN *ALFIE*, 2004

WHEN SAMANTHA GOT BACK to her hotel room after the ill-
fated trip to the airport, she was so overwhelmed by the
feelings swirling around in her head and heart that she didn't
know what to think. In one sense, she was proud of herself for not
backing down. She'd stood her ground and given Aidan a piece
of her mind. Yet at the same time, she felt sad that she had been
duped again by Aidan.

Normally, Samantha would have called Sydney to tell her all
the unfortunate details of what had happened. But she just couldn't
face the inevitable "I told you so"—Syd had never approved of
Aidan. So instead of reaching out to anyone, Samantha opted to
spend the day exploring the city. She didn't need Aidan to have a
good time in San Francisco.

* * *

Sydney and Gavin enjoy the perfect day . . .

On a whim, Gavin and I decided to see a Twins game. He'd still never seen the home team play, so I thought it would be a bit of local fun. Just as we made our way to the upper deck—let the hardcore baseball fans pay the big bucks for closer seats; we just wanted to be in the ballpark—my cell phone rang.

Normally, I don't answer it when I'm with Gavin because we don't get to spend as much time together as we'd like, but it was Sam, and I hadn't talked to her in a while. I told Gavin to go on; I'd catch up with him.

"Hey, Sam," I said. "How's San Francisco? Isn't it amazing?"

"The city is incredible," Sam said. "But—"

"Honey, what's wrong?" I asked in my best sympathetic-big-sister voice. I can always tell when something's up with her.

"Things didn't go so well with Aidan," Sam said. "I wasn't going to call you because I didn't want to hear you say, 'I told you so.' But then I changed my mind."

"I would never say that, Sam," I said. "I love you too much. What happened?"

So Samantha proceeded to tell me everything. To say I was appalled would be putting it mildly. I was so angry that I wanted to fly out to San Francisco myself and give Aidan a piece of my mind.

"So where is Aidan now?" I asked. "He'd better not be anywhere near you."

"Don't worry, he's not," she said. "He's actually on an airplane back to Minneapolis."

"You're kidding," I said. "He just *left*?"

"Yep, he wanted to go home immediately," she said. "Can you

believe that? It's like he couldn't stand the sight of me."

"I wish I could fly out there and give you a big hug," I said. "I know it's not much, but you know I can relate to what you're going through."

"I know . . . the whole Liam fiasco," Sam said. "Did you feel like a fool for giving him a second chance?"

"Definitely," I said. "I felt like the lamest person on the planet. I just never wanted to see him for who he really was. I idealized him and thought constantly of his potential. But eventually, I realized his potential didn't matter if he was being one ginormous jerk. And he was. But that took awhile. I didn't get there overnight, that's for sure."

"I never understood what you saw in him then," she said. "But now I totally get it. You'd think I would've learned from your mistakes."

"Ha ha," I said. "No kidding. Guess you're a little slow."

"Slow, huh?" Samantha said, ribbing me a little. "But in all seriousness, I *have* to know something. Why did you encourage me to give it a try with Aidan when Eli was so good to me? That was really bad advice. Quite possibly the worst you've ever given me."

"I guess I felt like you needed to see Aidan's true colors—good or bad—for yourself," I replied. "You kept talking about him while you were dating Eli, wondering if there could still be something there. It wasn't a passing fancy. So that's why I said what I did. You could've stayed with Eli, but I'm not really sure he was your speed. There had to be something missing if you were so willing to dump him for Aidan."

"I see your rationale, but who are you to try to teach me a lesson about love?" she asked sharply. "Ever since you got married,

I think you've been a little out of touch with the singles' scene. You're in your happy little bubble with Gavin, speaking from experiences you had eons ago—"

"I had no idea that's how you felt."

"You know I love you—you're my sister and one of my dearest confidantes," Samantha explained. "But lately I feel like you're a little more interested in your own life and in meddling in the love lives of Jane, Lucinda, and whoever . . . and you don't really get what I'm going through. I think your advice about Aidan was a little flippant—"

"Flippant?" I asked, trying to remain calm, yet not really able to believe what I was hearing. She was getting more upset by the second.

"Yes, flippant!" Sam reiterated. "If I hadn't listened to you, I might just be in a functional relationship with Eli right now instead of heartbroken over Aidan."

"Sam," I said. "Sweetie. I'm so sorry if it seems like I was flippant. That wasn't my—"

"You know what? I don't think I want to hear the rest right now, Syd," she said. "I gotta go. I'll call you sometime soon." And then without any warning or even a good-bye, she hung up. She'd never hung up on me before.

Hot, salty tears started running down my face. As I made my way across the row to my seat, Gavin turned to me, concern in his eyes.

"What's wrong, baby? Why were you gone so long? Is Sam okay?"

"No," I said as I started to sniffle. With my foundation running down my face, I'm sure I was quite the sight to behold.

"Wanna get out of here and talk about it?"

"But we just paid for tickets to see the game," I said.

"Don't worry about it," Gavin said. "Besides, the game is really slow. We would've been bored out of our gourds."

Gavin always made me laugh. "Bored out of our gourds, huh?" I said. "Okay, let's get out of here."

As we walked downtown to grab a cup of coffee at Starbucks (Gavin assured me he'd go in so no one would have to see how hideous I looked, even though he said I didn't look any different than before), I told him all about what Sam had said on the phone.

"It was so hurtful," I said. "She has never said anything like that to me before. Not even when we were younger."

Gavin paused for a second, then spoke. "Sam's clearly in pain right now, so she's probably looking for someone to blame. It's much easier to do that than to admit you made a mistake."

"But what do I do next?" I said. "She sort of hung up on me."

"I'd give her some space and let her get in touch with you," Gavin said. "And we can pray about it in the meantime."

"Sounds like a great course of action," I said. "Thanks for listening."

"You don't have to thank me for listening," Gavin said. "That's what best friends do, my love."

❋ ❋ ❋

Lucinda embraces her inner domestic goddess . . .

On Saturday afternoon Lucinda had invited Philip over for a last-minute dinner, and he was thrilled by the unexpected gesture. To get ready, he picked up a great bottle of merlot and a bouquet of gardenias (Lucinda's favorite). He couldn't wait to see her.

Even as high maintenance as she could be, Philip really enjoyed spending time with Lucinda. In fact, he'd say he was pretty smitten. Lucinda was everything he wanted in a girl: She was beautiful, poised, funny, and smart—and that was just for starters. Philip also felt that their time together had been personally beneficial for both of them—just like individuals in any good relationship should, they brought out the best qualities in each other. For his part, Philip was able to trust again, and he no longer believed that his earlier failed relationships were his fault.

And Lucinda? She'd changed in so many ways. Since starting her relationship with Philip, Lucinda was a little less obsessed with her job and—even more surprising—a little less obsessed with herself too. Sure, she still wanted to look good, but she didn't feel the need to constantly change her hair color, get Botox, or exercise fanatically. Philip always made a point of telling Lucinda she was beautiful, and that made a world of difference for her sometimes fragile self-esteem.

Philip had also encouraged Lucinda to make a difference in the world, something that had always sounded better in theory than in actual practice to her. But Philip's example made it seem easy. She'd started sponsoring a child from Tanzania through a world relief organization and even served chili and cornbread at a homeless shelter with Philip on occasion. Moreover, it actually made her feel good—she never would've imagined—and she had him to thank for that.

With so much good at stake, she was understandably nervous about telling Philip what had happened at Bungalow 8. Philip was such a great guy, and Lucinda didn't want him to leave. Of course, she could have just forgotten about it. That kiss hadn't meant anything, and Philip would never know. But she felt compelled to be honest about it (a relatively new phenomenon for her) because she believed that she and Philip actually had a future. So secrets were absolutely out of the question. Now she just had to figure out how to broach the subject.

Lucinda paced in her apartment, waiting for the delicious Thai takeout she'd ordered for dinner to arrive. Because when it came to cooking, Lucinda had never been the envy of her friends. The last time she'd tried to cook (in a moment of utter optimism), she actually burned the water she was attempting to boil for a pasta dinner. Her friends told Lucinda repeatedly that that wasn't possible, but she had the charred pan to show for it.

Needless to say, Lucinda hadn't cooked since—a shame since her kitchen, complete with matching stainless-steel appliances, has Martha Stewart written all over it. But Lucinda and Martha are polar opposites. Nonetheless, Lucinda had become an expert at ordering takeout and making reservations. And if a home-cooked meal was required to impress a man (like tonight), Lucinda was adept at creating the comfy feels-like-home ambience.

Using the new maroon cloth napkins and matching placements she'd recently picked up at Pottery Barn and a tasteful centerpiece with vanilla-hazelnut candles, Lucinda's dining room table looked elegant and chic. Thanks to the candles, the room smelled rather beguiling too, something Philip pointed out when he arrived a few minutes later.

"Well, look at this! Your place looks like it should be in *House Beautiful* or something," Philip said as he wrapped his arms around Lucinda's waist and gave her a kiss. "It even smells heavenly."

"Thanks for your vote of confidence," Lucinda said. "I guess what I can't do in the kitchen, I make up for in home décor."

"That's right, you don't do kitchens," Philip said. "Didn't you burn water once? Or was that just a nasty rumor?"

"Not a rumor, sadly," Lucinda said. "I ordered Thai for tonight."

"Fine by me," Philip said. "If we get married, I guess I'll do the cooking and you'll do the cleaning?"

"Or you'll do the cooking and I'll hire a maid," Lucinda said with a laugh.

"I could live with that," Philip said with a huge grin on his face. "Now let's eat. I'm starving!"

❋ ❋ ❋

Aidan's plane is beginning its descent into Minneapolis/St.
Paul . . .

As Aidan looked out the small airplane window, he'd never been so relieved to see the familiar Twin Cities landmarks. To say the vacation with Samantha was a disaster was putting it mildly. But it was also a wake-up call.

Aidan simply wasn't ready for a romantic relationship at this juncture of his life. He knew that now. When he was in India, he'd begun to feel like he was finally figuring out who he was. But as soon as he'd returned from that environment, where his role was clearly defined, he'd been unmoored. And when he began to wonder what life could be like with Sam again, everything spiraled out of control. When that "I love you" slipped out of his mouth, he'd known he'd made a mistake. Unfortunately for Samantha, Aidan turned out to be exactly what she'd most feared when she began dating him again. Aidan knew this too, but he wasn't sure how to remedy it. An apology simply wouldn't be enough. But Aidan believed that just as her wounds had healed the last time he'd made a fool out of himself, she'd heal again. And instead of forcing himself back into her life, causing confusion for all parties involved, he now knew to stay far, far away. And to pray for Samantha whenever he could.

As soon as Aidan got back home, he also planned to give his two weeks' notice and head back to India—where he knew he belonged (and wished he'd never left).

※　※　※

Flipping channels in San Francisco . . .

Samantha knew that staying in and watching television was a little lame in a city as breathtaking as San Francisco, but as hard as she tried, she simply couldn't muster up the energy to do anything else.

She hoped there would be some sort of good escapist television show or movie on the tube but was disappointed to discover that her TV only had seven channels. Therefore she was forced to decide between watching an episode of *Family Guy* or a rerun of *America's Next Top Model*. C'mon, where was a good chick flick like *My Big Fat Greek Wedding* when you really needed it?

As Samantha flipped endlessly through her limited amount of programming, she thought of Sydney. Sam knew she'd been a little tough on her today, and at some point she was going to apologize—but tonight wasn't going to be the night. Sick to death of nothing good on TV and suffering from a battered heart, she decided to turn to someone she'd been too distracted to be in contact with lately: God.

Opening up the drawer to the bedside table, she took out the Gideon's Bible and began to read one of her favorite books: Jeremiah. The irony of this, of course, was that Samantha was looking for encouragement from the man known as the weeping prophet. She always found comfort in this flawed man, though. At least Jeremiah was always man enough to admit it (hmmm, maybe Aidan could take a cue from him).

One verse in particular in chapter 29, Sam's favorite, always stuck out, and she turned to it for comfort: "'For I know the plans I have for you,' declares the LORD, 'plans to prosper you and not to harm you, plans to give you hope and a future.'"

Those words were especially encouraging tonight because Sam's future seemed anything but certain. She now had no boyfriend, no career, and no idea of what the future might bring. So she held on to God's promise and a smidgen of hope.

✽ ✽ ✽

Coming clean with Philip . . .

So far, dinner at home with Philip was going great. But Lucinda was about to drop the bomb. She ate the remaining bite of spring roll on her plate and decided it was officially time to face the music.

"Remember when I told you I had something to tell you?" Lucinda said as she turned to Philip.

"Yeah," Philip replied. "And I've been worried about that because it sounded a little portentous."

"Portentous?" Lucinda said. "That's a twenty-five-cent word if I've ever heard one."

"I've got to keep the big-time magazine editor on her toes, right?" Philip said. "But you're stalling, honey. What's up?"

"I know, I know, I *was* stalling," she began. "And it's because I care about you so much."

"You can tell me anything," Philip said reassuringly. "Whatever it is, it's going to be fine."

"Okay, here's the deal," Lucinda said. "I had this work function the other night at Bungalow 8—"

"Yes, I remember," Philip said. "I couldn't go."

"Yes." She paused again, but Philip just waited patiently.

"I was at the club, and I ran into a guy Sydney interviewed for *Vogue*," Lucinda said. "She'd wanted to set me up with him. Before you and I ever went out."

"Okay. So?" Philip said, looking a little confused.

"I'm not quite finished yet," Lucinda explained. "I was having sort of an existential crisis because I've never been as happy as I have been with you. So I put it to the test and—"

"And?" Philip asked quizzically.

"And I kissed him," Lucinda said. "But it didn't mean anything! It was a mistake! I made a horrible mistake."

"Wow." Philip shook his head. "So you just kissed this random stranger to see how you felt about commitment? That's a dangerous experiment."

Lucinda hung her head, her eyes tearing up. "It was awful."

"I don't like the thought of you kissing anyone but me."

"Me neither," Lucinda said. "Think you could forgive me?"

Philip paused for a moment, then spoke. "I know you could've just hid this from me. But you chose to tell me—which tells me that you care."

"I do," Lucinda said. "Without a doubt."

"So please don't do it again," Philip said. And he smiled.

"Deal," Lucinda said. She smiled too. "I won't make the same mistake twice."

208

CHAPTER 17

SUNSHINE OR SNOWSTORMS? TAKE YOUR PICK.

Maybe something terrible will happen — maybe you'll have a good time.

— HUBBELL GARDNER (ROBERT REDFORD) IN *THE WAY WE WERE*, 1973

SHERYL CROW ONCE SANG that a change would do you good. Maybe it was the song's sheer repetitiveness or the fact that Sheryl wasn't one of her favorite singers, but Jane had always hated that song.

Yet when it came time to decide whether she wanted to accept the job in California or stay at KARE-11 in Minnesota, that maddening refrain was stuck in a perpetual loop in her head. Three weeks had passed, and the song was wearing out its welcome.

Maybe that annoying song was a little sign to guide her. Or maybe it was just a coincidence that she kept thinking of it whenever she tried to make the best decision. But that song—along with the promise of eternal sunshine and practically having the ocean in her backyard—is what clinched the deal for Jane. She was moving to California.

And the job wouldn't be bad either. After getting used to

a familiar routine at KARE-11, the new position would offer a variety of new challenges, particularly an opportunity to flex her writing muscles.

She wasn't so excited about having to make new friends. She'd be losing Campbell (not that there was much to lose, but he'd been a friend), and she would really miss Sydney. It was rare for Jane to have close girlfriends, and now she'd be leaving the best one she ever had. But at least all was not lost: Sydney traveled to Los Angeles a couple of times a year for work, so it wouldn't be long before they'd be shopping on Rodeo Drive and catching up on all the news. Or at least that's the thought Jane consoled herself with.

* * *

Everything's changing for Sydney too . . .

There are a million things I love about Minneapolis, and autumn is easily in my top ten. It arrives in late September and is gone in the blink of an eye, but while it's here, it's truly magical.

And today was one of those perfectly picturesque days. The changing trees were a palette of rusts, oranges, and yellows; the air was clear and crisp like the flavor of a tart green apple. It's the weather of sweaters and football games, and I couldn't believe it was going to be my last in Minnesota.

It's amazing how much life can change in only three weeks.

After a good long run in the Twin Cities, I was officially Tennessee-bound: Gavin had been accepted to Vanderbilt for the spring semester, so we were going to be heading there after Christmas.

And even though I had some rather interesting (for lack of a better word) memories in Nashville—that's where I'd met Liam—I wasn't going to hold that against Music City. This time I was going to be with the love of my life, so the whole situation was bound to be better, right?

I sure hoped so.

There was so much to do before we left, though. First off, we had to sell our cute little condo. I'd bought it before I met Gavin, and even though it probably wouldn't seem like much to most people, it sure felt like home to me. And apparently the price was right because we'd already had three people who'd come to see it. Strangely enough, I was thrilled when none of the couples wanted to take the place. They just didn't *oooh* and *aaah* like I hoped our condo's future owners would.

Gavin thought it was a bit, well, odd that I felt this way, but I rationalized it by saying that the condo and I went way back. I wanted someone to appreciate the care I took to make it a place worth coming home to after a long day of work.

And I believed we'd still find that very person—or couple.

When I wasn't dreaming of who'd be crashing at our place when we were long gone, I was searching for apartments on Rent .com or answering letters for "Lucy for the Lovelorn." The column had gotten even more popular since I'd taken over (always a compliment) and was carried three times a week now.

It was a lot of work, and I was finding it difficult to be insightful and clever all the time. The other day I'd ended up staring at my computer screen for the better part of an hour trying to figure out what to say to a guy who thought his significant other was from another planet (and trust me, he wasn't merely suggesting that she was from Venus in the funny self-help way).

Eventually I found my groove, though, and today's batch of letters was particularly giggle inducing.

> *Dear Lucy for the Lovelorn,*
> *I'm feeling a little pathetic today because everyone I know is dating someone, and I'm not. Even my troll of a brother, who doesn't do anything but play Xbox all day, has found someone. What should I do so I will no longer be repulsive to the opposite sex?*
> *Help!*
> *Marci, Seattle, Washington*

> *Darling Marci,*
> *You live in an amazing city where cute guys are probably as close as your local Seattle's Best Coffee. So get out of the house and don't worry about your troll of a brother. After all, can his relationship really be all that great with an Xbox mistress in the picture? Yeah, I didn't think so. Have you left the house yet?*
> *Love,*
> *Lucy*

This one cracked me up too.

> *Dear Lucy for the Lovelorn,*
> *My boyfriend bought me a blender for my birthday. Do you think he's thinking of proposing soon?*
> *Anastasia, Springfield, Illinois*

Darling Anastasia,
If that blender's in the shape of a diamond ring,
then yes. Otherwise, he might just think you've got
a thing for smoothies.
    Love,
    Lucy

Every time I read one of these letters, I thank God I'm not single. But despite what Samantha said, I feel like I do have some valuable insight on the subject because not so long ago, I was walking in their shoes. All the "Lucy" letters have inspired me to write a book on relationships, something I began last week.

I'd had an idea for a quirky novel awhile ago, but it just wasn't taking shape. So I left that alone and started exploring this new idea, and the words flew so freely that I'd written twenty or so pages in no time flat.

As I was writing, though, I found myself thinking about Samantha and how she's been doing. She hadn't asked me to pick her up from the airport. And she still hadn't called me since she hung up on me that day. It wasn't like Samantha not to call me back, but I continued to give her some space until she felt like talking. It wasn't particularly easy—not in the least.

✴ ✴ ✴

Aidan decides to make things right . . .

All the details for a return trip to India came together much more quickly than Aidan could've ever imagined. He was leaving in three days, and he knew that before he left the country again, he needed to make something right.

This sudden change of heart concerning Samantha came from a few long meetings with his pastor. Even though Aidan hadn't felt like he'd really done anything wrong, his pastor was quick to correct him. Then rebuke him. Then give him some advice. And after several in-depth conversations, he was finally convinced and couldn't believe he'd been so woefully insensitive.

At first, Aidan considered e-mailing. But Sam would probably delete it, and e-mail didn't seem quite personal enough, anyway. So he went to Target and picked up a funny greeting card that made a joke at the expense of men. Hoping that would break the ice a little, Aidan considered his words carefully.

Then he started writing:

> *Dear Samantha,*
> *I'm leaving for India in just a few days, and I've finally come to a full realization of how much of a jerk I've been. I know you're probably thinking that I'm a little slow in figuring that out, but better late than never, huh? Coming to terms with what I did has been one of the most challenging things I've ever dealt with, and I only hope in time you'll be able to forgive me.*
>
> *I want you to know that I do care about you, but I've realized that I'm incapable of having a healthy and functioning relationship. I've got so much to learn about love and relationships, and I hope that you'll pray for me as I explore all of that.*
>
> *Again, I have you to thank for my love of*

*India, and I will never forget that. I pray that
God will lead you as you pursue the next leg of
your life's journey.*

    *In the meantime, God bless. I'm praying for
you too.*

    Aidan

After Aidan signed his name and sealed the envelope, he knew he'd done the right thing. But would Sam even read it? Or would she see his name in the return address section and immediately rip it up? He didn't know, but he could hope for the best.

❋ ❋ ❋

Dealing with the Sunday blues . . .

Sam started a new job as an administrative assistant at a psychiatry office in downtown Minneapolis last Monday. While the work was mundane and really just a means to an end for now (after all, it didn't take a college education to file, copy, and make sure the doctors had the files they needed before patients came to visit), it paid reasonably well and helped her stay afloat financially until she decided what to do next.

As ambivalent as Samantha felt about the new position, though, she could still feel the onset of a major case of the Sunday blues. She just wasn't ready for another week to start. From time to time, a good mope session was what a girl needed, and that's exactly what she'd done most of the weekend. Devouring seemingly endless amounts of Ben & Jerry's Chunky Monkey ice cream. Listening to loads of sappy music of the Kelly Clarkson persuasion. Looking at pictures of herself and Aidan, then promptly ripping them up into a million little pieces. You know, the typical postbreakup girl stuff.

But as fun as that all was, Samantha knew she had to move on at some point. It just hadn't been quite as easy as she'd expected. Maybe she'd try out that singles' group that Sydney had always talked about. Maybe being among other people going through the same thing would be therapeutic somehow. In the meantime, there were still a few good moping hours left and a carton of Chunky Monkey waiting for her in the kitchen.

❋ ❋ ❋

Breaking the news to Sydney . . .

While I watched the Packers game (Favre was having his best season yet!) with my laptop perched on my knees, my phone rang. Not a day went by now when I didn't hope Samantha would call, so I quickly grabbed it. My caller ID indicated it was Jane.

"Hi, Sydney," the cheery voice said.

"Hi! What's going on?" I replied. "Enjoying your Sunday afternoon?"

"I am—especially because I'm officially going to be a California girl," Jane said.

"That's so exciting!" I said with a squeal.

"I know!" she said. "You'd better come and visit."

"That's a no-brainer, girl," I said. "You know how much I love LA."

"Good," she said. "I'm a little nervous about making friends there. I mean, can you trust a girl if her lips are all collagened up?"

I laughed out loud.

* * *

Breakfast and Tiffany's . . .

Philip had just finished off what had to be one of the most delicious breakfasts he'd enjoyed in a while. He'd found this old-time diner (and not one of those refurbished glossy joints) just a few blocks from his house. He couldn't believe he hadn't noticed the place before. The cook was a big believer in butter, which made Philip's order of eggs Benedict even richer than usual.

As he sipped his coffee and read the newspaper, Philip smiled when he thought about what he'd planned to do tonight for Lucinda's birthday. He was picking her up at five thirty: His church offered an afternoon service for people who liked to sleep in on Sunday mornings. Then after church, he was taking her back to his place, where he'd planned a romantic dinner. Unlike Lucinda, Philip knew his way around the kitchen pretty well—and thought her lack of kitchen skills was, well, cute.

For the past couple of days, he'd been checking out recipes online and had settled on a menu of lobster paella, steamed asparagus, and Lucinda's favorite carrot cake for dessert. Lucinda had specifically decreed that there be no candles on her cake (she was vain about her age . . . Rome wasn't built in a day, right?), so that was duly noted.

After breakfast, Philip was headed to Tiffany's. He didn't

know what it was about women and those robin's egg blue boxes, but Philip knew you couldn't go wrong with a gift from Tiffany's.

* * *

Blast from the past . . .

As Samantha polished off the carton of Ben & Jerry's—a rather impressive feat, if she did say so herself—she heard her phone ring. Since she was boyfriendless, there was no reason to have a special ring tone anymore; every call was announced by Pachelbel's "Canon in D."

She didn't recognize the number or the area code. Where was 617 from?

"Hello?" she said curiously.

"Hi, Sam, it's Eli."

Samantha nearly dropped her phone at the sound of his voice. Was Eli really on the other end of the line? Why was he calling from that strange area code?

"I'm guessing from your silence that you're a little shocked," he said.

"Um, a little, yes," she said. "But it's nice to hear from you."

"Well . . . I don't know why today had to be the day," Eli began. "But I wanted to let you know that I'm not mad at you anymore."

"Thanks," Samantha offered weakly, not really knowing how to respond. "I would've been mad at me too."

"It took me awhile to get to this place," Eli said. "But there's something about a new start that's liberating."

"What exactly do you mean by a new start?" Samantha asked.

"I moved to Boston," Eli said. "It's one of the best things I've ever done. I have a job that I love. A church that I love, and—"

"Boston?" Sam asked. "What made you choose Boston?"

"A song actually," he said. "Long story."

"I'm really happy for you, Eli," she said. "You deserve every happiness."

"So do you, Sam," Eli said.

They didn't talk much longer. And somehow Samantha knew that she and Eli probably wouldn't keep in touch after that. He was in Boston, after all. It just didn't make any sense to. But she was okay with that. She and Eli had closure, which was one more giant step in moving on with her life.

❋   ❋   ❋

It is the happiest birthday of all for Lucinda . . .

Lucinda was never a huge fan of birthdays. If she'd had her way, she would've stayed twenty-eight forever. But despite the fact that she was turning . . . well, that's not important (a woman never reveals her age, right?), Lucinda was having an incredible time with Philip. And so far they'd only gone to church.

Today's sermon was about taking leaps of faith, and that's what Lucinda felt like she was doing with Philip, even though she hadn't known that when they'd started going out. Being with a guy who treated her well was the opposite of everything she'd ever experienced before. And while it took some getting used to, she rather liked the perks of a functional relationship. It was liberating to be free of all the drama she'd lived with before.

Now, back at Philip's place, Lucinda had never seen more loving attention to detail. Vases of gardenias were scattered throughout the room. Candles were lit, the table was set with napkins and plates in her favorite colors (celery green and ivory), and the smell of the lobster paella wafting through the house smelled scrumptious.

And while dessert was customarily the time for the events that were about to take place, Philip liked to keep Lucinda guessing—which wasn't always easy.

"I thought I'd go ahead and give you your first birthday gift," Philip said.

"The *first?*" Lucinda smiled. "I'm not opposed to that."

"You'd better not be opposed—because this is how it's going to be," Philip said authoritatively before cracking a smile. "Close your eyes."

Obediently closing her eyes, Lucinda waited as Philip fetched airline vouchers and placed them in her hands.

"Okay, you can open your eyes now," Philip said.

Lucinda looked down and spotted the tickets. "Two vouchers for a trip to Hawaii whenever we'd like!" Lucinda exclaimed. "That'll be incredible. Thank you sooo much, darling."

"You're welcome, sweetheart," he said, leaning forward for a kiss. "But that's not all."

Lucinda could barely hide her excitement. "You're spoiling me. A trip to Hawaii is plenty extravagant for a birthday."

"Well . . . this isn't just any trip to Hawaii," Philip said as he pulled the Tiffany's box from his pocket. "I want to get married in Hawaii, if you'll have me."

Then he bent down on one knee, opened the box with the

flawless three-carat diamond ring inside, and asked Lucinda to be his wife.

Lucinda had never been much of a crier, but the tears wouldn't stop rolling. If someone had told her that Philip was planning to propose today, on her birthday, she would've laughed.

"I would be honored to be your wife," Lucinda said.

"Good, good," Philip said as he slipped the rock onto Lucinda's ring finger. "I was getting a little worried there when you weren't answering."

"And I really like the idea of getting married in Hawaii," Lucinda said. "We won't have to spend two years trying to get the Plaza."

"I don't know what that means," Philip confessed. "But it sounds good to me."

As Lucinda looked at Philip smiling at her, she'd never felt happier in her life. She was going to be a bride and Philip's wife. It's almost like Sydney's need for carbs had saved her life. She couldn't wait to tell Sydney the news.

CHAPTER 18

CLEAN UP ON AISLE THREE, PLEASE!

Better bring out the big guns on this one. She's crazy with
a side of crazy!

—ALAN JOHNSON (DON CHEADLE) IN *REIGN OVER ME*, 2007

IT WAS A HAZY Monday morning in Minneapolis, and I wasn't
ready for the work week to begin yet. So I procrastinated on my
writing assignments by heading to SuperTarget in Roseville for
a little grocery shopping. Gavin and I were out of almost everything, so I figured it would provide at least an hour's worth of
diversion from my monstrous to-do list awaiting me at home.

After grabbing a Caramel Macchiato at the Starbucks in the
corner of the store, I walked through the produce section, my
favorite, to see what looked good. *Mmmm*, the peaches looked
especially good. And the organic raspberries and strawberries
would work for smoothies, while the apples would make a delicious
dessert for Gavin sometime this week.

Then when I was in aisle three, checking out the various pasta
options, something strange happened. I accidentally made eye
contact with this girl who'd been in the produce section at the
same time as I was, and she was now walking toward me. She
surprised me by saying, "I thought it was you."

"Do I know you?" I asked as I grabbed a couple of boxes of rotini and stuck them in my cart.

"You're Lucy," she said. "Lucy for the Lovelorn."

I had no idea I had fans. The picture that accompanied the column was only a thumbnail. How in the world did she recognize me?

"Well, actually, I'm Sydney," I said jokingly. "I just play Lucy in the newspaper."

But Mystery Girl didn't seem to find that particular joke funny. "I'm kind of mad at you," she said. "You told me to break up with my loser boyfriend, and so I did. And I've never been more miserable, thanks to you—Lucy, Sydney, whatever you want to be called."

"I'm so sorry to hear that," I said as sympathetically as I could. "So why do you feel that it was a mistake?"

"Because I miss him. Because he was sweet. Because—"

I jumped in. "I can't remember your exact letter, but if I told you to break up with him, I had a good reason based on something you said in the letter," I offered optimistically. "I don't just go and tell people to break up with their boyfriends for no reason."

"I forget what I said in the letter," she said. "I was just mad at him that day. And now he won't even speak to me, and it's *your fault*," Mystery Girl said, her voice growing loud enough to attract the attention of the other shoppers.

Trying to be as calm and rational as possible, I said, "You shouldn't write to an advice columnist just because you're mad at your boyfriend. Usually the problems I'm addressing are a little more of the long-term variety—"

"Oh, shut up," she said. "Your psychobabble isn't going to make this situation any better. You ruined my life, so now you get to live with that."

"Wait a minute," I said. "How could I ruin your life? I'm just an advice columnist. You can either accept what I say or let it go in one ear and out the other."

"Whatever," she said, turning to walk away. "I hate you, and all my friends do too." Mystery Girl wasn't paying attention to where she was going, and she brushed the endcap as she went by. A huge jar of Ragú promptly came crashing to the floor and shattered.

"Look at what you made me do, Lucy!" she said angrily. "Now *you* can clean it up." And she stalked off, leaving me to find someone to clean up the mess in aisle three.

I don't know what it was, exactly, but something seriously rattled me about that interaction. It wasn't technically my fault that she'd ended her relationship, but I still felt responsible somehow. Mystery Girl clearly wasn't happy with me or my advice and thought everything was my fault. That had been happening a lot lately: first with Jane, then Samantha, and now a complete stranger. Maybe meddling in people's relationships wasn't all it was cracked up to be.

❋ ❋ ❋

While I was still trying to figure out what I could've done differently with Mystery Girl, my cell phone rang. Great, it was Lucinda. What in the world could she want me to do now?

"Hello?" I said in a slightly annoyed tone.

Lucinda wasted no time responding. "Well, hello to you too. Just so you know, that's not the way you talk to someone who's engaged!"

"Lucinda!" I said. "I'm so happy for you. Guess Philip wanted it to be a very happy birthday, huh?"

"Yeah, I was knocked-off-my-booty surprised," she said. "And you know me, I'm rarely surprised."

"I *do* know that," I said. "So what kind of ring did he get you?"

"Big," she said. "From Tiffany's."

"I'd expect nothing less for you," I said with a laugh. "If someone had told me six months ago you'd be getting married, I would've laughed. But with Philip, I can totally see it. You are going to be so happy."

"Awww, thanks, Syd," Lucinda said. "Why does everything make me cry lately? I just teared up there."

"Maybe you're just caught up in an amazing moment," I said.

"Whatever it is, it better stop. I have to buy new mascara every week now."

Now that sounded a bit more like the Lucinda I knew and loved (and sometimes just tolerated).

"A small price to pay for happiness," I said. "So when's the wedding?"

"I've been meaning to ask you about that," Lucinda said. "Want to be my matron of honor?"

If there was ever a woman destined to be Bridezilla, it was Lucinda. But I couldn't say no, I just couldn't.

"I'd be happy to," I said. "As long as you don't drive me crazy in the process or make me wear anything crocheted."

"Crocheted?" Lucinda asked.

"Long story," I said.

"By the way, I'm getting married in Hawaii, so you might

want to start laying off the carbs," Lucinda informed me. "The dresses are going to be light, airy, and gauzy."

"Gauzy, huh?" I said with a laugh. "Sounds like I'm going to be wearing a gigantic bandage."

"You were always better with words," Lucinda said. "But you get the gist, right?"

"Got it," I said.

"So we'll want to meet sometime next week to start discussing everything from the flowers to the catering to the—"

"Hey, Lucinda," I said. "Don't you want to just bask in the glow of your engagement a little longer? Like maybe give it a week at least?"

"Oh, I suppose you're right," Lucinda said. "But there's going to be so much to do that I figured we might want to get an early start."

Which is exactly what I was afraid of.

"Sydney—you still there?" Lucinda asked when I was silent for, oh, four seconds.

"Yep, still here," I said.

"Have I ever thanked you for setting me up with Philip?"

"I think you probably have."

"In case I haven't, I want to thank you again. Philip changed my life."

"I know he did, and for that I'm grateful."

"Hey, what's *that* supposed to mean?"

※　※　※

Filing papers gives one time to think . . .

As always, the downtown office where Samantha worked was a hoppin' place—even before noon on a Monday. Not only was it a revolving door of patients, but Mondays were when all the mandatory staff meetings took place, leaving Samantha with a whole lot of coffee orders to fill and papers to file.

But the mindless activity did have its advantages. It gave Samantha plenty of time to think. When she was filing a brief about a new psychiatric program in Prague, it made her nostalgic for Europe. She had done her internship there the summer after her junior year, and to say the experience was a life-changing one would be selling it short. It was one of the most incredible times of her life, and now she wondered if there were any career opportunities there. Samantha made a mental note to check into that later.

Meanwhile, her boss, Mr. Phillips, was calling. "Sadie, Sadie?"

"It's Samantha actually," she said politely.

"I'm sorry about that," Mr. Phillips said. "I had an ex-girlfriend named Sadie, and she sort of reminds me of you."

Ick, Samantha thought. The idea of Mr. Phillips dating made Samantha feel slightly nauseated. He was a big, burly old man who'd pass more for a professional wrestler than a psychologist. But that was just appearances, of course, she reminded herself primly.

"What can I do for you, Mr. Phillips?" Samantha asked.

"I'd like you to show our new employee around," Mr. Phillips said. "His name is Austin, and he just moved to town after his tour of duty in Iraq. Maybe you could take him out to lunch or something. He is an American hero, after all."

Love the subtlety, Mr. Phillips, Sam thought. *Why don't you just come out and say you want me to date him? He's probably about as exciting as—*

"Hi, I'm Austin," he said, extending his hand to shake.

Struck speechless from the sight of Mr. Tall, Blue-Eyed, and Handsome (that's TBH for short), Samantha shook his hand. "So I hero that you're—"

"I'm your hero, huh?" Austin said. "And you haven't even gotten to know me yet. That's mighty brave of you."

"Let me try this again," Samantha said, blushing a little. "I hear that you just moved to town."

"Why, yes, you're right, I did," Austin said. "Know anywhere good to have lunch?"

"Actually, Mr. Phillips suggested we do just that. Guess he's treating," Samantha said.

And before she could even fully process it, Samantha and TBH were off to grab a bite to eat, which didn't bother her in the least.

* * *

Settling in with the Food Network . . .

As Rachael Ray made another one of her tasty thirty-minute meals in the background, I was lying on the couch, curled up with a blanket. Since I had a rather lenient boss—myself—I'd taken the rest of the morning off to ponder its events.

In the case of Lucinda, who was now happily engaged, my participation in her love life resulted in a three-carat ring from

Tiffany's—and more important, the promise of true joy as the wife of Philip. That, along with the setup of Rain and Stinky Nate, which also resulted in holy matrimony, meant I have made two very successful matches. Since things are still going well between Kristin and Justin, I've actually made three couples happy. And all the positive letters I get from "Lucy for the Lovelorn" readers indicate that I'm doing a world of good, right?

So if that's the case, why does it bother me so much when my advice doesn't pan out? Should I quit matchmaking while I'm ahead? Or should I continue, knowing that another psycho grocery shopper who felt he or she got bad advice could be lurking in the produce department? Or aisle three? I was seriously going to have to give this some thought.

CHAPTER 19

TO DATE OR NOT TO DATE, THAT WAS THE
QUESTION

> You gotta have a boyfriend, don't you? Otherwise it's just
> you and a cat and before you know, 40 candles on your
> birthday cake.
>
> —NOELLE (UMA THURMAN) IN *THE TRUTH ABOUT CATS & DOGS,* 1996

LUNCH WITH AUSTIN HAD been unexpectedly fun for Samantha—maybe the most fun she'd had in a while. He was probably five or six years older than her and already had led such an exciting life.

As they shared sushi, he told her about his time in Iraq and how grateful he was to be back in the States. And since so many soldiers have such a difficult time readjusting to postwar life, Austin was excited to be using his counseling degree to help them deal with it. If he was going to be working in an office setting, he desperately wanted to do work that mattered—something Sam could definitely relate to.

When the conversation turned to hobbies, Austin and Samantha discovered they shared a lot in common: They both loved the outdoors, they both loved to travel, and they both didn't mind shopping, although Austin wasn't exactly the shoe horse that Samantha was—not that that was surprising.

Their rapport was comfortable, which made Samantha feel at ease, even though they'd just met. And as Samantha stared intently into his piercing blue eyes, she began mentally debating the politics of dating a coworker. Most people would call it a bad idea, but Samantha wondered if she could be the exception to the rule. *Okay, probably not. But hey, this is only a temp job anyway.*

Not that she had to worry about that yet. Austin hadn't exactly invited her on a date. But if he did, she'd have a very difficult time saying no. Samantha knew that for sure.

❋ ❋ ❋

Boys will be boys . . .

Jane thought it was funny (and not in a ha-ha way) how guys were sometimes. Here she'd been around for months and months crushin' on Campbell, and all they'd done was flirt. And now that Jane was moving to Los Angeles soon, Campbell unexpectedly decided to ask her on a date. Seriously, what was the deal there? Was Jane "safe" now because Campbell knew she was leaving? Or was it because she had stopped going to group that she was no longer a threat? While she would've accepted immediately a few months ago, she now had to think this one over. Did she want to go on a date with Campbell? Or had his expiration date arrived the day he gave her the whole I'm-sorry-if-I-gave-you-the-wrong-idea speech?

Jane wasn't sure, and it was something she had to get to the bottom of before she called him back.

✳ ✳ ✳

Samantha's in her own little world . . .

After her lunch date—scratch that, her welcoming-Austin-to-the-company outing—Samantha was surprisingly giddy. There hadn't been a guy who appealed to her in weeks; the only men in her life at the moment were Ben and his friend Jerry. Always loyal, they were there whenever Samantha needed them. But with her pants getting more snug by the day, it was good that Austin was around to distract her. He was a great calorie-free option.

Helping Austin get set up in his office, Samantha made sure he had all the office supplies he needed, the phone extensions of everyone in the company, and the special code to get soda for free from the vending machine. It didn't take long for Mr. Phillips to notice her attentiveness.

"My, my, my, Samantha," Mr. Phillips began. "I didn't see you give Holly this much attention when she started. But I do appreciate you getting Austin up to speed on everything. Nice work."

Samantha turned to Austin. "I'm not sure if you're aware of this, but Mr. Phillips is pretty heavily medicated," she said. "He tends to just ramble and mumble and say things he doesn't mean."

"Hey! I heard that," Mr. Phillips said.

Austin smiled at Samantha. Apparently none of this worried him in the least. He didn't mind Samantha's attention one bit.

❋ ❋ ❋

Back in the saddle again . . .

Deciding that I couldn't worry about what was already in the past, I decided to press forward with my work. I mean, there's only so much of the Food Network you can watch before you start feeling pretty lazy. Or hungry.

Speaking of hungry, I knew Gavin would be home soon, so I started considering what to make for dinner. But in the meantime, I got a burst of creative energy, so I decided to make the most of it by wrapping up a few deadlines.

Just as I pressed send, I got a text from Samantha. My long-lost sister. I KNOW, I KNOW, YOU THINK I'M DEAD. BUT I'M NOT. HOPE YOU'RE DOING WELL. MET A CUTE BOY TODAY. WILL 'PLAIN MORE LATER. — SAM

So I guessed that meant Sam was going to call sometime in the not-so-distant future, a fact that made me want to jump for joy. Literally. It had been way too long.

❋ ❋ ❋

Movie date or no movie date?

So here's the deal: Campbell had asked Jane if she'd like to see a movie. Tonight. Not in a group, not for a singles' group outing, but *on their own*. Granted, Jane had to be at work bright and early, but it might be worth it to hang out with Campbell. Going to a movie with him wouldn't be a big deal time-wise. But how did she feel about going out with him from an emotional standpoint?

That was where everything got a little fuzzy.

Even though she was frustrated with Campbell's reasons for turning her down earlier, she still appreciated the opportunity to get everything out in the open. She understood it and had moved on. But now Campbell wanted to go out all of a sudden? That was a little strange.

Was she flattered by the attention? Absolutely. Did she still think Campbell was attractive and definitely datable? Well, yes . . . aside from the fact that she was moving to Los Angeles and Campbell was in Minneapolis. But hey, stranger things have worked out, right? It's never been easier to keep in touch, even across the miles.

So after her what's-Campbell's-endgame? rant was over, Jane decided a movie sounded good. It would get her out of the house.

❋ ❋ ❋

Two sisters reunite . . .

As soon as Sam got off work, she dialed Sydney's number. She was a little nervous. Strange, since she was calling her sister. But after the long silence between them, Sam knew she had some explaining to do. Big-time explaining.

But as soon as she heard Sydney's warm voice, her apprehensions were immediately put at ease. It was as if no time had passed at all.

After a tentative hello, she began to apologize for the long, long gap between calls.

"Don't worry about it, Sam," her sister said. "I'm just glad we're talking now. The past is behind us."

"I was a little harsh," Samantha said. "I'm sorry about that. I was definitely having issues."

"No explanation necessary," Sydney said.

Then Sam filled her in on Austin (Syd labeled him "a tasty new development").

"So do you think you'd go out with him?" Sydney asked.

"Well . . . do you think it's bad to date someone from work?" Samantha asked.

"Dating a guy from work is never the best idea," Sydney said. "But if you really like him, you could always get a new job, right?"

"It's not like I plan to be there forever," Samantha said.

*　*　*

Campbell arrives right on time . . .

Since there weren't a lot of appealing options at the regular movie theaters, Campbell and Jane decided to head to the Roseville 4, a budget theater, to catch something they hadn't seen during the first run. It wasn't exactly a glamorous first date, but it wasn't a big deal—they felt like old friends.

Campbell picked Jane up at seven o'clock for a seven thirty showing. And because there weren't any previews, they had plenty of time to pick up ice cream at the grocery store right next door, since they'd agreed on the phone that they weren't really in the mood for movie snacks.

After they each settled on a container of Ben & Jerry's, Campbell paid for the ice cream, and Jane snuck in the containers in her oversized purse. Since it was her brand-new limited edition Prada bag (a celebratory splurge), she was secretly praying that the ice cream wouldn't leak. Yes, it was a vanity prayer, for sure, but Jane believed that God cared about the little things too—like ice cream dripping all over your $1,200 purse.

Once settled in the cozy airplane seats that leaned all the way back and provided a bunch of legroom to boot, Jane handed Campbell his container of B & J and one of the plastic spoons she'd retrieved from the deli.

Jane thought that being out with Campbell would be more awkward than it was, considering the frank conversation they'd had about their feelings. But it really wasn't. They chatted quietly until the movie started and then watched without interacting much—save for jostling for position on the armrest.

Afterward, Campbell asked her if she'd like to get coffee or a snack. Appetizers sounded good, so Jane agreed. And that's when they were really able to talk.

"May I ask you a straightforward question, Campbell?"

"Sure," he said. "I have an idea of what you might ask, but I'm curious how you'll word it." They smiled at each other.

"Okay, here goes: Is it really about the chase?" Jane asked. "I mean, I practically spelled out my feelings for you, but you gave me this big speech about why it wouldn't work, and now a short time before I'm about to move over fifteen hundred miles away, you ask me out. Explanation, please?"

Campbell laughed. "That was about what I expected," he said. "I'd like to say it was some devious master plan. But when I heard you were leaving, I realized that I didn't want you to go without getting to spend an evening with you first. I *have* thought about you, I always have. I guess I was just—"

"Just what?" Jane asked.

"A little intimidated. I felt unworthy of you," Campbell said. "I'm sure you've heard that before and don't consider it a compliment. But you're a strong, beautiful woman, and I was a bit taken aback by that. I usually go for the lightweights, just so you know."

Jane laughed at his candor. "At least you're honest."

"It's an unfortunate characteristic of mine."

"I wouldn't call it unfortunate," Jane said, touching his arm, a telltale sign that she liked him.

"You wouldn't, huh?" Campbell said. "Guess that's two points for me."

"Oh, I don't know about two points," Jane said. "Maybe one."

And that's when Campbell leaned across the table, gently pushed her hair away, and kissed her, much to Jane's surprise and delight.

* * *

Lucinda just can't wait . . .

Not long after I hung up with Sam, my phone rang again. *I am quite the popular girl tonight . . .*

"Sydney, it's your favorite bride," Lucinda said with a tone so cheerful I almost thought it wasn't her.

"Yeah, I gathered that from the caller ID," I said sarcastically.

"Oh, did someone wake up on the wrong side of the bed?" Lucinda asked.

"Nope. Just been a long day. You know how that goes."

"Not lately, but in theory, yes," Lucinda said, before launching into what she wanted to talk about.

"So I know that we wanted to let me have time to bask in my engagement, but trust me, I've basked," Lucinda said. "I'm so ready to start planning the wedding now. Right now."

Now there was the Lucinda I know and love. Her first word as a child probably wasn't *mama*—I have no doubt that it was *now*! Of course she wanted to plan the wedding now. Instant gratification was Lucinda's middle name.

"So what exactly were you hoping to accomplish tonight?" I asked. "It's way past business hours."

"Oh, I know that, silly," Lucinda said. "I just thought we could get some sort of exploratory meeting in the works and talk about the details of my engagement party."

"Exploratory meeting?" I asked. "Are we planning a wedding or staging a coup?"

"You're hilarious, Sydney," Lucinda said. "You know a wedding is a big deal. People are expecting me to have a lavish affair."

"What about you and Philip? What do you want?" I asked.

"Philip wants whatever I want. He knows I'll want something over the top," Lucinda said. "I'm only planning on doing this once, so I want it to be truly memorable."

I was glad to hear she was only planning on doing it once. Wouldn't it be horrible going into a wedding thinking it wasn't going to work? But I guess people do that all the time.

"That's good to hear, Lucinda," I said. "So where are you thinking of having your engagement party?"

"What do you think of Nobu?" Lucinda asked. "It would be chic without being too showy."

"So you're thinking Japanese food is the way to go?"

"What would you suggest, a ton of carbs?" Lucinda said. "The guest list is mostly going to be staff from *Vogue*, models, and actors, so they could actually eat sushi. Not too many calories."

Point taken. Does the whole carbs joke really never get old to her?

"You're probably right," I said. "No one wants to get fat going to someone's engagement party. It's important to know your audience, right?"

"Yep, just like writing," Lucinda said. "Incidentally, I think that's a pretty good start. Wanna meet soon to discuss the rest?"

"If you want to fly me there, then yes," I said. "If not, the phone will have to do."

"Oh yeah, that's right—you don't live here," Lucinda said. "And what's this I hear about you moving to Tennessee? That's ghastly."

"Ghastly, huh?" I said. "At least I'll be further east. A little."

"That's something," Lucinda said. "Now you just need to go a few hours north."

"I know, I know," I said with a laugh. Lucinda was as persistent as ever. "I'll give you a call next week. Sound good?"

"Fine, darling," Lucinda said. "Cheers."

Once again I wanted to remind Lucinda that she wasn't British, but why bother? She was happy, she was planning a wedding, and I'd agreed to help for reasons I'm not even sure of. Sigh.

WELL, TOMORROW IS ANOTHER DAY

It's about me and him, not about us and other people.

— SARA JOHNSON (JULIA STILES) IN *SAVE THE LAST DANCE*, 2001

IT DIDN'T SEEM POSSIBLE that we were already saying good-bye to Jane. When I woke up this morning, I had a hard time holding back my tears. Thankfully, I had Gavin there in close proximity to comfort me.

"It'll be all right, I promise," Gavin said as he stroked my hair. "We'll make sure you get out there to visit her. Lots."

I sighed. "Who am I going to do Pilates with?"

"I'd like to think it could be *me*—but I just don't think I'm cut out for Pilates," Gavin said.

The sincere look on his face made me laugh out loud. "I'd pay money to see you do Pilates. You'd be adorable."

At least he had the grace to blush as he threw off the covers and got out of bed.

For the past week or so, Gavin and I had been planning Jane's party for tonight, Halloween night, so she'd still have a few days reserved for packing before she had to leave for the City of Angels.

Instead of opting for the traditional going-away party, Jane had suggested a Halloween costume party. A costume party isn't really my bag (or Gavin's either), but I knew this party wasn't about me. It was about Jane, so Gavin and I sucked it up and bought our costumes at a nearby thrift store. And just to make things extra dramatic, we decided to go as Scarlett O'Hara and Rhett Butler. While Gavin was from Texas and didn't have much trouble with a Southern accent, my attempt was less than stellar, so I decided to be Scarlett without the accent.

Too bad I couldn't be Scarlett without the hoop skirt. It was pretty uncomfortable, even when I was trying it on at the store, but I still thought the dress (a near replica of the one Scarlett made out of curtains in the movie) was absolutely killer. I simply had to have it.

Gavin was definitely less enthusiastic about his pencil moustache and vintage Rhett Butler look, but he rationalized that it was only one night and that if anyone made fun of him, he could just blame me, saying, "My wife dresses me funny."

But the person who was happiest about the party was Jane. After her last-minute date with Campbell that night at the movies, they'd decided to navigate the dating waters, as tricky as that would be when they were in two different cities. Despite their chemistry, they promised each other they'd take it slow and just see how things ended up once Jane got to Los Angeles. And if it didn't work out? They vowed to stay friends nonetheless.

Just as I'd guessed when I wanted to match them up in the first place, Jane and Campbell are an adorable couple. Campbell is cute and protective of Jane, while she is clearly overjoyed at having him in her life, even if everything is still in the beginning stage. And tonight, she was particularly excited about their costumes: They were coming as Romeo and Juliet as an homage to her high school years when she'd played the lovely lead in the school play.

And if that wasn't enough for me to get excited about, Samantha was also planning to bring Austin. While they hadn't made their relationship official, they had been spending an awful lot of time together. I mean, going out night after night practically qualifies as dating to me, but Samantha and Austin were in no rush to label themselves as boyfriend and girlfriend. And after what happened in her previous relationships, I definitely can understand why Samantha's a bit gun-shy.

In addition to her friends from KARE-11, the singles' group had also been invited, something that made Campbell a little nervous when we all discussed the party initially. But his feelings for Jane had begun to deepen over the past couple of weeks, and I think he got to the point where he didn't care as much what they thought. It would be an interesting night.

＊　＊　＊

I decorated our place with several jack-o'-lanterns I'd carved (complete with votives inside to illuminate their faces), corn stalks, and bales of "hay" I'd picked up at Michael's craft store. The hay was a bit messy and unwieldy, but it really completed the earthy fall vibe I was going for.

For nibbles, I'd made Jane's favorite lime punch (it was a lovely, intense shade of green) and a few light appetizers. With Gavin's help, we had everything in order by seven o'clock, a minor miracle, considering it took me at least an hour to get into my Scarlett ensemble.

But now with every last pin curl in place and my best *fiddle-dee-dee* to greet all the guests, I was ready for the party to start.

Naturally, the guest of honor showed up first, arriving hand in hand with Campbell. Their Romeo and Juliet costumes were elaborate but looked far more comfortable than ours, which secretly made me a little envious.

"You guys look great," I said with a grin. "Have some punch, make yourself at home, and if you'd like, choose some music from the iPod."

"Sure thing," Campbell said, and he made a beeline for the music.

"Everything looks really nice, Syd," Jane said from across the room. "Thanks so much again for having this for me."

"Of course," I said. "It's our pleasure. Well, minus this hoop skirt. I don't know what I was thinking there."

"Just be glad it's not a corset," Jane said. "Life could be much, much worse."

"You're right, girl, it could be."

* * *

"Sorry I'm a little late," Samantha said as she and Austin walked in. "I got off work late, went home to change, and realized I had nothing to wear for a costume party."

Remembering that Sam's last costume party experience hadn't gone all that well, I said, "No worries, Sam" and then gave her a hug. "It's just so good to see you; I've missed you."

"You too, sis," Sam said. "Oh, by the way—this is Austin."

Playing it cool like I hadn't heard much about him, I shook his hand. "Great to meet you, Austin," I said. "Can I take your coat?"

"Sure," Austin said. "Anything I can do to help?"

I liked this guy already. Sam so needed to quit her job—and fast.

As Austin made his way to the living room, I winked at Sam and mouthed, *He's really cute.* Sam smiled and whispered, "I know" before she joined Austin on the couch.

Then a bunch of people from the singles' group slowly trickled in. Most of them were girls, and a few weren't exactly subtle when it came to offering their opinions about Campbell and Jane. As I refilled the punch bowl in the kitchen, I heard one girl whisper (but not quietly enough) to another, "Why do you think he'd date her anyway? She's leaving and will probably date, oh, I don't know, Leo DiCaprio or something."

"Nah, I don't think she's pretty enough to date a celebrity," the other one said. "And I personally don't think she's good enough for Campbell either."

This exchange reminded me that girls are catty. And while I so wanted to say something to let them know I'd heard every gossipy word they'd said, I silently kept refilling the punch bowl.

* * *

Unlike those high school dances you might remember that always went on a smidge too long, Jane's going-away party passed by at a pretty speedy clip. After everyone ate and mingled a bit, Jane opened her presents, which included several gift certificates so she could decorate her new LA digs in style. Her rent was going to be double what it had been in the Twin Cities, and she wasn't going to have much extra cash for home décor, so everyone pooled their money and got her gift cards (which are always easier to pack than regular gifts too) from Home Depot,

Macy's, IKEA, and Target.

"Thank you so much, everyone," Jane said sweetly when she'd finished reading her cards. "It means so much to me that all of you would want to say good-bye. I'm going to miss you terribly."

Yeah, well, my guess is that a few girls in the group were ready for her to be gone. One girl in particular, Marissa, spent the majority of the night not so discreetly staring at Jane and Campbell. Finally, toward the end of the evening, Campbell asked Marissa if something was bothering her.

"I just think it's wrong for you to date anyone who even used to be in the group," Marissa said defensively.

"I'm sorry you feel that way," Campbell said with a smile. "But I really like her, and I don't care who knows it. Maybe in time you might find it in your heart to be happy for us?"

Campbell's bold declaration of how he felt about Jane elicited a few claps from the crowd, but as you might expect, Marissa promptly made her way out.

"I'm certainly not going to miss her," I said to Jane jokingly.

"Yeah, I don't think I am either," Jane said. "Isn't Campbell just—"

"Yes, he is! I'm so glad it ended up working out between you."

"And I'm so glad you suggested we'd make a good couple," she said. "Even if it took forever to work out."

I laughed as Campbell walked up behind her.

"Ready to get going, babe?" Campbell asked. "I've got an early morning meeting with Pastor Steve—as in six o'clock. Brutal, isn't it?"

"That Pastor Steve," Jane said with a laugh. "Okay, I'll grab my coat and we'll get out of here."

As Jane and Campbell made their way out, the majority of the other guests followed, leaving Samantha and Austin and a couple of girls from the singles' group behind to hang out with Gavin and me.

"Want to play Taboo?" I asked. It's one of my favorite word games, but you need several people to make it fun.

Unfortunately, no one else shared my enthusiasm for the game. "Why don't we watch a movie?" Samantha suggested as an alternative. "Syd and Gavin have a pretty incredible DVD collection."

"Now that I could go for," one of the girls said enthusiastically. "Where are your movies so we can check 'em out?"

"They're on a shelf in my office—second door on the right," I said. "Bring out a few options so we can all decide on one."

Then, as we all waited for the girls to select a few movie possibilities, I noticed Austin put his arm around Sam, a sight that made my heart burst with happiness. Not only was Sam back in my life, but here she was in our living room, enjoying a new relationship with someone who's actually her speed and seems like a pretty great guy. I'm hoping Austin stays that way—for Sam's sake and mine. And if doesn't work out? Well, at least I won't have had anything to do with it—a major relief for a meddler like me.

CHAPTER 21

THE DOCTOR IS OUT!

Any questions? Don't ask. I'm tired of talking to you and I
want to sleep.

— MR. WHITE (TOM HANKS) IN *THAT THING YOU DO!*, 1996

TODAY WAS THE FIRST day I went to Pilates class without Jane.
She left town four days ago — November 6, to be exact — and
I was already missing her.

I had no one to get calorie-laden smoothies with after we'd
worked so hard in class. I also had no one to snicker with when
Stella Barkley, a seventy-four-year-old grandmother in our class,
constantly complained that her pancreas hurt after every set of
stretches we completed. Without a doubt, my back, arms, and
calves hurt after every Pilates session . . . but your pancreas? That
was just too funny. I couldn't tell you where my pancreas is located
if my life depended on it.

Despite desperately wanting to stay home from class, I decided
that I'd better get used to the fact that Jane wasn't going to be
around anymore. She'd been driving the last few days, but by now
she was probably in Los Angeles, enjoying the sunshine and starting
this new chapter of her life. At least she had something to show for
her time in Minneapolis: a wonderful boyfriend. Life was pretty

sweet for my much-missed friend.

After showering and changing into clean clothes, I packed up my MacBook and headed over to Moose & Sadie's. Since I was writing my last "Lucy for the Lovelorn" column today, I desperately needed a change of scenery. Home just wasn't going to cut it today.

As excited as I had been about being Lucy in the beginning, the proverbial fairy dust had worn off in a hurry. There'd been a recent batch of letters with problems so complex that I had to write twenty of them back personally with recommendations for places to get real advice. And after the bizarre confrontation at the grocery store, I was exhausted. So instead of continuing to complain about it, I finally gave my editor my notice.

While some of my fellow journalist friends didn't understand why I would give up the opportunity to ghostwrite a syndicated column (opportunities like that don't come knocking very often), I tried to explain the burden that comes with getting involved in the love lives of strangers. It was bad enough when people I love, like Sam and Jane, were angry with me. But when readers across the country started confiding their deepest, darkest relationship secrets to me and asked for my help, I couldn't stop thinking about what happened after my column was published. Did things get better in their lives? Or worse? Some let me know (and in painstaking detail), but most of them didn't.

These definitely weren't the lightweight matchmaking problems that Emma had to deal with, that's for sure. The more time I spent writing the "Lucy for the Lovelorn" column, the more I was becoming an unpaid version of Dr. Phil. It was a lot of responsibility, which wasn't nearly as fun or appealing as I'd thought it would be.

* * *

Here comes the bride . . .

In a moment of sheer frustration while she was trying to decide between an ivory strapless wedding dress or a snow white one with spaghetti straps, Lucinda chucked her big-wedding dreams out the window. Literally.

All these wedding details were driving her mad, and she hadn't even bothered to consult with Sydney yet. So with one swift movement, she strode from her living room to the window, opened it, and threw her copy of *Brides*, along with all her relevant notes inside, out the window. Thankfully, no one was hurt in the process.

Pitching the magazine was even more therapeutic than she'd expected—so therapeutic, in fact, that she called Philip immediately to tell him the change of plans.

"Hi, honey, whatcha up to?" Lucinda asked.

"I'm finishing up the business plans for the Minneapolis Pinkberry store," he said. "How about you? I'm sure you're doing something far more exciting."

"I just whipped all our wedding plans out the window," she said.

"You just *what*?" Philip asked. "Should I be worried?"

"No," she said. "You should be happy. I want to elope. I've decided this whole big-wedding thing is overrated. I just want to be with you."

"Seriously?" he asked, still in a state of disbelief. "That's what you want?"

"Absolutely," she replied. "Maybe we can take our matron of honor and best man, our families, and that's it."

"I love how you think, Lucinda," Philip said. "This may be

the best plan you've ever had."

* * *

So long, farewell . . .

After careful tweaking and about two hours of hard labor with some major procrastination mixed in, I finally finished my last "Lucy for the Lovelorn" column. Breathing a huge sigh of relief, I read it over one last time.

> *Dear Lucy for the Lovelorn,*
> *I started dating my best friend about six months*
> *ago, and in the beginning, it was everything*
> *I wanted. It seemed to be the culmination of*
> *unrequited feelings we'd both had for a long time.*
> *But now that we've been dating for six months,*
> *the spark is gone. There's not one clear-cut thing*
> *he's doing wrong; there's just a bunch of little*
> *things that annoy me to no end. It's nothing*
> *criminal, but I can't help but think that this isn't*
> *going to work for the long haul. How do I know if*
> *it's the right time to leave?*
> *Stacie, St. Louis, Missouri*

> *Darling Stacie,*
> *Ever hear the expression "curiosity killed the*
> *cat"? Sure you have, and I suspect that's what*
> *may have happened here. While friendship is the*

ultimate foundation for a functional, healthy relationship, it sounds like you and your best friend may have simply been better as friends. And even though these annoyances you reference are nothing criminal, apparently they were enough to warrant writing in, so I'd have the talk with your boyfriend ASAP.

And speaking of knowing when to fold 'em, readers, you're going to be hearing from a new Lucy the next time you read this column. The time has come for me to pursue other opportunities, but I thank you for sharing your lives with me. It's been a pleasure.

Love,

Lucy

Really, it was a fitting way to end my run as an advice columnist. I did know when to fold 'em, and the time was now. While being a modern-day Emma has provided its share of joy, there have been plenty of teachable moments. Meddling in the love lives of your friends and family has serious consequences if not handled with the utmost care. And no matter how much fun it is at the start, it's certainly not worth losing a friend over.

And with that final sign-off, I bid Lucy (and Emma) farewell for good. I'll always give advice about love—it's in my nature. But for now, I won't seek out any new matchmaking opportunities. Instead, I'll pray that my friends (and even Mystery Girl) will find true love. Sure, Emma might be a little disappointed with my plan, but I know plenty of people (especially Gavin) who won't be.

Now back to my regularly scheduled article for *Vogue* . . .

etc.

bonus content includes:

READER'S GUIDE

1. After Jane's disastrous date with Weston, why do you
think she's so eager to have Sydney set her up again?
2. When Sydney suggests setting up Campbell, the singles'
pastor, Gavin questions whether that's a good move.
Do you think that, by definition, a singles' group leader
should also be unattached? Why?
3. Do you think Samantha made the right decision in
accepting the gift from Aidan when he unexpectedly
turned up at Applebee's? Or was that unfair to Eli?
4. Does it surprise you when Lucinda says she might try
to find a guy at a local church? Do you think she has a
chance of meeting someone her speed?
5. Given Samantha's past track record with Aidan, do
you think Eli has a reason to be worried about their
relationship when Aidan comes back into the picture?
6. Like Jane, have you ever done something that was out of
your comfort zone (like leading a Bible study, in her case)
in hope of impressing a guy you have a crush on? Was the
tactic successful?

7. What's your gut reaction when Eli overhears Samantha confessing her feelings to Aidan? Do you think Samantha got what she deserved when Eli unexpectedly showed up?

8. Do you think Mystery Guy has enough going for him in the exchange at the bagel shop to warrant Sydney's setting him up with Lucinda? Why?

9. Even though it's way beyond the call of duty, why do you think Sydney is willing to breach journalistic etiquette to see if Elton is available to date Lucinda? Do you think Lucinda would really fire Sydney if she didn't?

10. Would it be difficult for you not to be a superfan if you were interviewing the cast of your favorite TV show or movie? Why?

11. Why do you think Gavin has such a hard time writing songs from a happy place? Is joy really such a difficult emotion from which to create compelling art?

12. When Philip suggests a coffee date for his first date with Lucinda, she thinks it's because he "doesn't want to shell out the big bucks until he meets me for the first time." Is meeting for coffee a lackluster first date?

13. Even though it wasn't the career step she was hoping for, do you think Jane was right in accepting the job in Los Angeles?

14. Do you agree with all of Sydney's "Lucy for the Lovelorn" advice? If not, which specific instances are problematic?

15. When Gavin was offered a chance at a publishing deal, do you think he should have given it a shot? Why?

16. Why do you think Lucinda finally opts out of having a big wedding?

17. After everything Samantha went through with Aidan, do you think she's ready for a relationship with Austin? Why?

18. What do you think Sydney has learned from her experiences in meddling? Do you think her days as a modern-day Emma are really over?

SYDNEY'S RECOMMENDATIONS FOR LIFE'S LITTLE CIRCUMSTANCES

SYDNEY'S TOP TEN BREAKUP SONGS

When you need to wallow, these tracks will help you indulge your breakup blues.

1. "Everybody Hurts," R.E.M. (1992)
2. "I Will Survive," Gloria Gaynor (or the hilarious cover from Cake) (1978, 1996)
3. "La Cienega Just Smiled," Ryan Adams (2001)
4. "Special," Garbage (1998)
5. "Since U Been Gone," Kelly Clarkson (2004)
6. "Shiver," Coldplay (2000)
7. "Don't Think of Me," Dido (1999)
8. "Someday You Will Be Loved," Death Cab for Cutie (2005)
9. "Which Will," Nick Drake (1972)
10. "One," U2 (1991)

SYDNEY'S TOP FIVE MAKEUP SONGS

When you find love again, these songs revel in the romantic bliss.

1. "Ice Cream," Sarah McLachlan (1994)
2. "Forever My Friend," Ray LaMontagne (2004)
3. "Let's Fall in Love," Frank Sinatra (1960)
4. "More Than Anyone," Gavin DeGraw (2003)
5. "You're the Ocean," Teitur (2003)

etc.

DO SOMETHING!

If you're like Gavin and want to help promote music education, check out these tried-and-true resources.

- VH1's Save the Music Foundation at http://www.vh1 .com/partners/save_the_music/
- The Guitar Center Music Foundation at https://www .guitarcentermusicfoundation.org/
- The Mr. Holland's Opus Foundation at http://www .mhopus.org/
- Global Music Project at http://www.globalmusicproject .org/
- Sound Art at http://www.soundartla.org/
- MIMA Music at http://www.mimamusic.org/

ABOUT THE AUTHOR

CHRISTA ANN BANISTER has worked as a respected music critic and freelance writer for various Christian publications, including *CCM Magazine*, Crosswalk.com, *Christian Single*, and ChristianityToday.com. Christa lives in St. Paul, Minnesota, with her husband, Will. They love to play Scrabble and throw darts on a map and dream about someday going wherever the darts land. And until her books hit the *New York Times* bestseller list, Christa is happily employed as a freelance writer for her many, many clients.

Additional great titles from the NavPress fiction line!

Around the World in 80 Dates
Christa Ann Banister
ISBN-13: 978-1-60006-177-6
ISBN-10: 1-60006-177-X

Travel writer Sydney Alexander is ready for one particular journey to end: her frustrating search for a Mr. Right. But things are looking way up. Just after landing her dream job, she meets an eligible round of bachelors, including a dashing European, a promising blind date, and a charming coffee-shop wordsmith. Now Sydney will discover just how far she's willing to compromise to land her dream guy.

Match Point
Erynn Mangum
ISBN-13: 978-1-60006-309-1
ISBN-10: 1-60006-309-8

Lauren Holbrook, matchmaker extraordinaire, takes credit for four successful couples now. With her dad happily married and life settling down around her, Lauren feels quite content. That is, until the tables are turned and she's on the receiving end of the matchmaking!

Bottom Line
Kimberly Stuart
ISBN-13: 978-1-60006-077-9
ISBN-10: 1-60006-077-3

As much as she loved being home for Nora's first steps, words, and forays into makeup artistry, Heidi misses working, not to mention money for pedicures. And her husband, Jake, seems increasingly worried about their dwindling bank balance. So when the beautiful Kylie Zimmerman, with a wave of her multi-carat–laden fingers, dangles the chance to become part of a "life-enhancing, woman-affirming business opportunity," Heidi takes the bait. What does she have to lose?

To order copies, visit your local Christian bookstore, call NavPress at
1-800-366-7788, or log on to www.navpress.com.
To locate a Christian bookstore near you, call 1-800-991-7747.

NAVPRESS ⏻.